Done Darkness

A collection of stories, poetry, and essays about life
beyond sadness.

Edited by Pam Parker and
Kathy Lanzarotti

Orange Hat Publishing
www.orangehatpublishing.com - Waukesha, WI

www.orangehatpublishing.com
Waukesha, WI

We dedicate this publication to all who struggle with the dark curtain of depression or other mental imbalances. We hope that in some of these pieces our readers may see themselves, or loved ones, and understand that they are not alone.

Kathy Lanzarotti and Pam Parker

From the Editors

Pam Parker

Sadness, anxiety, grief, depression – these issues can affect any human being over the course of a lifetime. But, we don't always like to talk about depression or other mental illnesses. Why then choose to compile an anthology about life with and beyond sadness?

I've lived with depression requiring medication for over seven years. Previously, especially in a grief-stricken time in college, I dealt with it in unhealthy self-medicating ways. In my family background, I'm aware of two suicides, active depression, one lobotomization in the 1950s, bouts of alcoholism (some treated, some not), cases of bipolar disorder, and a healthy sprinkling of ADHD. I'm painfully aware that my family fits the mold of many in the U.S.. While both genders and all socioeconomic levels face these issues, women are more likely to seek and follow through on treatment than men. Statistics bear this out again and again. When Kathy and I put out our call for submissions, we were inundated with pieces from women. We briefly considered making the anthology only with pieces from female authors, but decided against it. We wanted to remain open to whichever pieces offered the most diverse viewpoints and experiences that we could. Mental imbalance doesn't affect only one gender, race, or religion. It's an opportunistic invader open to all humans. I hope *Done Darkness* may spur discussion, tolerance and perhaps even someone seeking treatment who could benefit from it.

Done Darkness is not meant to be used to treat anyone's illness. But hopefully, in these stories, essays, and poems, readers will find voices and feelings to connect to, to gain a better understanding of their own experiences or perhaps of a loved one. My greatest hope is that someone experiencing the cloud of deepest darkness, will believe, and know, that hope exists. That the light can and will return.

Kathy Lanzarotti

Done Darkness is not a clinical journal. It is instead, a collection of shared stories and experiences. These stories, essays and poems reflect the daily battle with various forms of depression: clinical, postpartum, and reactive, just to name a few. My hope for this collection is that our readers can find something in these pieces that echoes their experience and that they can find some comfort in the fact that they are not alone. That others have been down that singular dark well and have worked their way back in to the sunlight.

Depression is an invisible illness. There is no rash, no limp, no tremor. There is just interior emptiness, helplessness and distress. It is an intensely personal experience that affects roughly ten percent of Americans in some form. With these numbers, it is very likely that you or someone you know is effected by it. If I may take a line from the war on terror, if you see something say something. If someone you know seems to be in pain, is acting erratically or appears to be in need, ask if they're okay or if they need help. Show you care. Let them know that they are not alone and that this thing, depression, does in fact exist. Sometimes it's the most seemingly insignificant act of kindness or interest that can change a person's outlook, can make their day, and maybe even save a life.

Done Darkness

A collection of stories, poetry, and essays about life
beyond sadness.

Orange Hat Publishing
www.orangehatpublishing.com - Waukesha, WI

Previously Published Pieces

Jason Lee Brown's poem, "Intersection," first appeared in *Midwestern Gothic, Issue 3.*

Sarah Cooper's poem, "Lymph Nodes, Liver Lesions and My Mother," was originally published with *Melancholy Hyperbole.*

Litsa Dremousis's essay, "Neurological New Year's Logic" first appeared in *The Weeklings* as "Neurological New Year's Logic" and in *Salon* as "My Terrifying Chemical Storms".

Amy Hassinger's story, "A Smart Bug" first appeared in *Arts & Letters, Issue 29.*

Jody Hobbs Hesler's story "Nature of the Sun" appeared originally in *The Blue Ridge Anthology 2013,* from Cedar Creek Publishers.

Kathy Lanzarotti's story, "Have You Seen Me?" was published in *Creative Wisconsin, Fall 2012.*

Katie Manning's poem, "Why Are You Depressed, He Asks" was published in *The Southwestern Review.*

"Bificuration" from *Healing With Words: A Writer's Cancer Journey* by Diana M. Raab. Copyright (c) 2010. Used by permission of Loving Healing Press, Inc.

"Shadow Texts" by Mike Smith first appeared in *Witness Vol. XXVIII, No. 2.*

Dallas Woodburn's "The Man Who Lives in My Shower" was previously published in *Zahir: A Journal of Speculative Fiction.*

Special thanks to all members of our editorial review board:
Gessy Alvarez
Amber Dermont
Max Garland
Carolyn Healy
Tony Press
Carol Wobig

Table of Contents

Morning

Afternoon

Evening

Baptism
by Claude McKay

Into the furnace let me go alone;
Stay you without in terror of the heat.
I will go naked in--for thus ''tis sweet--
Into the weird depths of the hottest zone.
I will not quiver in the frailest bone,
You will not note a flicker of defeat;
My heart shall tremble not its fate to meet,
My mouth give utterance to any moan.
The yawning oven spits forth fiery spears;
Red aspish tongues shout wordlessly my name.
Desire destroys, consumes my mortal fears,
Transforming me into a shape of flame.
I will come out, back to your world of tears,
A stronger soul within a finer frame.

Morning

"You think your pain and your heartbreak are unprecedented in the history of the world, but then you read. It was books that taught me that the things that tormented me most were the very things that connected me with all the people who were alive, or who had ever been alive."

—James Baldwin

Done Darkness

A Smart Bug
by Amy Hassinger

"It's *my* turn!" William's voice rose up from the basement, making Josie pause in her kneading to listen for whether his voice had reached that certain pitch, the one that meant she'd better quit whatever she was doing and get down there, fast. It hadn't, not yet.

"They'll figure it out," she told her friend Mary, who was perched on the stool across the counter, sipping a beer. Grains of flour clung to the blond hair on Mary's forearms. "Go on, I'm listening."

"There was a shard sticking out of the man's eye," Mary continued. "Straight out. He couldn't close his eye at all. The nurse was squeezing saline into it so it wouldn't dry up."

"Christ. Are you trying to make me puke?" Josie pulled the dough toward her shelf of a belly and folded one corner over, smooshing it with the heel of her hand.

"Maybe." Mary giggled the same way she had at fifteen whenever Josie caught her in the middle of some mischief: disappearing behind the lunch tables with a boy at the school dance, for example, or drinking from a cup of "juice" that reeked of rum.

"I already puked my guts out this morning, okay? Seriously. I don't need any inspiration."

"Poor Jose. Still puking into the second trimester." Mary tipped back the bottle again, its base ridged in flour.

"Just another way I'm deficient."

"Oh, come on, Jose. That's not what I meant."

"That's what it sounded like." She knew she was being crabby, but couldn't help it. Late afternoon sunlight angled through the window, making Mary's skin glow amber, like the beer. Even with hair plastered to her head and blotchy cheeks, Mary was too bright to look at. Josie turned away, folding over another corner of the dough. "How'd he get the glass in his eye, anyway?"

"Usefulness."

"What do you mean? That doesn't make any sense."

"He was trying to install a new mirror in his bathroom when one of his kids chucked some toy at it and the thing exploded in his face. That's what you get for being useful—a shard of glass in the eye." Mary set the bottle down, empty.

"That's what you get for having kids," Josie countered. She looped a floured finger around the neck of the empty bottle and set it in the sink. "You want another?"

"Frank'll think I'm a lush."

"You are a lush." She dumped the handful of flour on top of the layer of squeezed-out juice boxes in the garbage can. "I'll tell him I drank it." She took another bottle from the fridge door, its neck cold between her fingers.

"Then you'll get in trouble." Mary picked the church key off the flour-dusted counter. An empty shape remained, outlined in flour. "Or more trouble than you're already in."

Josie glared at Mary.

"Just teasing, Jose."

Josie wanted that beer, badly. There was a time when she and Mary would have jogged together, and would now be sweating and drinking as equals, flanking this counter on just this sort of afternoon.

"*I* get to be the undertaker now!" William again, his voice nearing the edge. Soon there would be violence.

Mary laughed. "Your kids are the only ones I know who play 'funeral home.'" She took a long pull on the new bottle. Josie watched her swallow, feeling a ghost of the fizzy yeast on her tongue. *This is the way it goes and goes,* she thought. *There is more and more of them and less and less of me.*

She slid open the oven drawer, and pulled out a baking pan, clanging it against the other pans with more noise than necessary. Standing, one hand on her lower back, she crashed the pan against the stovetop.

Mary raised her eyebrows.

"Sorry," Josie muttered. She sprinkled cornmeal on the pan. At the counter, she shaped the dough into a loaf. "So, what? Are you against usefulness now? Is that the moral of the story?"

"Maybe." Mary's steely-blue eyes flashed. "Maybe I am. People are too goddamned useful. Look at you—baking bread, having babies, teaching kids things, creating all kinds of hazards, left and right. You need to quit it."

Josie rolled her eyes, acknowledging the joke, the patronizing back-handed compliment. Usefulness, she knew, was precisely the way Mary measured a person's worth: a person was admirable in direct proportion to how useful they were to the world. And Mary, as an ER physician, was clearly the more useful of the two of them, though Mary would never in a million years admit it. Lately, Josie had begun to feel that her choice to stay home with the kids had curbed her own usefulness. Over the last six years, her life had narrowed and thinned, and was now defined almost entirely by the boundaries of her own body and the walking, talking, screaming, whining extensions of that body. Her life had thinned, but her body had swollen and was now outsized, an embarrassment, spreading itself over its own boundaries like a loaf left to rise too long in the pan.

"I've got to empty the compost," she said.

Leaving Mary at the counter with her beer, Josie stepped out the back door, the pail of compost heavy in her hand. Their dog Delilah ran ahead of her. The weather had been strangely warm for March—hitting eighty just the other day—so that already the redbuds and shadberries and magnolia trees had flowered and fallen, leaving carpets of slimy petals on the sidewalks. The daffodils were on the verge, yellow buds pushing their life against the green. Josie had planted peas and spinach last week, and already they were up, the shoots greening above the black soil. Creeping Charlie and quackgrass were colonizing the beds; she would have to get on her knees with a hand hoe tomorrow and wreak some devastation. She waddled past the garden to the fenced compost pile behind the garage, where she dumped the contents of the pail. The grapefruit rinds tumbled over the strawberry tops and carrot heads and garlic peelings, making a colorful, pungent heap. She felt her gorge rise for the third time that day, and turned away, toward the treehouse, breathing through her mouth.

A spiderweb stretched from one corner of the treehouse ladder to an overhanging branch. Its strands winked gold in the afternoon light and trembled in the breeze, ringing octagonally out from the center of the web, where the spider waited, her body heavy and round, her legs marking her station in perfect stillness. Josie was reminded of *Charlotte's Web*. She and Gracie were in the middle of it at bedtimes. Just last night, they'd read the part when Charlotte tells Wilbur about how she sucks the blood—or, really, the liquefied innards—of the insects she catches in her web. "Is that true, Mama?" Gracie had asked, and Josie had stopped and told her all about spiders: how they actually paralyze their prey first with venom so they don't feel any pain, and how it might seem vicious and bloodthirsty to Wilbur and to us, but really, that's just the way they were, and that they were actually good in another way, since they ate things like mosquitoes and biting flies. How the earth needed all kinds of creatures in order for everything to be in balance. "Charlotte can't help being a spider," Josie had said, echoing E.B. White. "That's just the way she is. Just like Delilah. Delilah can't help chasing after squirrels and baby bunnies. That's her nature."

"Like William," Gracie had added contemplatively. "He can't help saying all those bad things he says. That's just the way he is."

Now, Josie stepped closer to the web and blew on it, making the whole thing sway, its strands stretch and rebound. The spider stayed poised in the center, unfazed. Spiders must know the difference between a breeze-vibration and an actual bug-caught-in-the-web vibration.

The cool thing about being a spider, Josie thought, as she waddled back to the house, was that you got to rebuild your whole world whenever you felt like it. One day you could reign over the kingdom of the treehouse ladder, the next you could colonize the garden fence or the lamppost or something. When things got to be too much of a drag, you just up and moved. And when your babies were born, they just dropped a line of web and flew away on the first available breeze.

Josie's foot met with something sharp and she pulled it away, expecting to see broken glass, a rose of blood blooming on her sole. But it was only a pebble she'd stepped on—a yellow angular pebble with sharp edges. Just the sort of thing Gracie would love. She would make wishes on it and add it to her collection. Josie squatted to pick it up, then crawled around on her knees, pawing the grass for some equivalent treasure she could offer William. He was less picky; just about any pebble or stick would do, as long as he got something, too. She found a chip of concrete, slipped it and the pebble in her pocket, and heaved herself to standing.

Back inside, she stepped into the sound of the children raspberrying one another in the basement with malicious gusto. As if they'd been waiting for her, there came a sickening thud and then, a keening scream. Mary appeared, beer in hand, her worried face relaxing at the sight of Josie. "Oh, good," she said. "I was—"

But Josie was already lumbering down the stairs. William, his little three-year-old fists clenched, stood above Gracie, who was sobbing in a heap on the floor. Josie swept William up in her arms and carried him upstairs. "Time out for you," she said.

"I am not allowing to punch Gracie," he shouted, pummeling Josie's back.

"That's right, William," she replied. "No punching. No punching and no hitting in this house." She carried him over to the living room couch, where she deposited him. "You stay there until I say you can get up."

"I hate you, Mama!" William yelled at her back as she went to see about Gracie.

But Mary was coming up the basement stairs with Gracie on her back, Gracie's skinny legs wrapped around Mary's flat belly. Gracie's face was wet, but she was smiling and her eyes were bright. Still, when she saw Josie, she reached out, and Josie reached back, taking Gracie—who was six and over fifty pounds—in her arms. Her lower back twinged. Gracie tucked her head beneath Josie's chin and took Josie's collarbone in her mouth, a habit she'd picked up as a baby. Josie nuzzled her head.

"No broken bones," Mary said. "I think she'll be okay. Right, Gracie?"

Gracie nodded, her face still buried in Josie's skin.

"I don't know about your mom, though. Carrying big kids like you around like that. You might do her in, Grace."

Gracie looked worriedly up at Josie, who smiled, betraying none of her pain.

Mary took a last sip of her beer, set it in the sink next to the other bottle and strode toward the door, her perfect cellulite-free thighs moving freely beneath her running shorts. A few strands of her hair lifted in the sunlight, filaments as golden as the spiderweb outside.

"I'm off," she sang, in a voice ringing with self-possession, a voice that astonished Josie with the sound of its own freedom, its ability to leave a room, a house, a family behind, and to move forward according to its own rhythm, its own whim, whenever and wherever it pleased. "Thanks for the refreshment of body and soul, Jose. Give me a buzz this week—maybe Frank'll let you out for a bite or something."

"Yeah, okay," Josie returned, letting Gracie slide over her belly to the floor. "I'll call you."

"Bye, Mama Mary!" Gracie yelled.

"Bye, Princess Grace," Mary winked, pulling the door shut.

Josie and Grace went into the living room, where they stood

side by side, watching William pull a thread from the hem of his pants, unraveling the stitching with total absorption.

"Say you're sorry, William," Josie instructed. "Then you can get up."

"Sorry," he replied automatically. He didn't even remember what he was apologizing for, Josie knew, but it didn't matter. Gracie had forgotten, too. She was now experimentally lifting the dog's leg, seeing how far she could go before Delilah raised her head and nudged Gracie with her nose, her warning.

William jumped down from the couch and went to Josie. She squatted, let him climb onto her belly and lace his arms around her neck, and then stood, using her leg muscles as much as possible. She kissed his moss-soft cheek, buried her nose in his apple-y neck.

"Lean, Mama." He pushed her away from him, toward the wall behind. "Lean."

"Like this?" She rested her upper back against the wall so that William was riding her belly as if she were the green dinosaur in the grocery store, the one you could ride for free, the one he would sit on for hours if she let him, pushing the start button again and again.

"Yeah." His face settled with satisfaction. "Like that." And she rested her upper back against the wall, her lower back pinching in pain, while William rode the swell of her belly.

Then, just under his thigh, the baby kicked—a swimmy, squirmy nudge. William's eyes got big and he grew still.

"Did you feel that? The baby kicked you."

He nodded back at her with quiet awe. Then, climbing off her belly, he ran to Gracie, who was already looking up from Delilah's bed, having heard every word. "I felt the baby!" he shouted. "The baby kicked me in Mama's belly!"

Gracie and William both ran over to Josie, who slid down the wall and sat on the floor. "Let me feel," Gracie insisted, and she snuggled in close, resting her hand and then her cheek against Josie's belly. William scrambled back on top of her, hugging her with his legs, trying to recreate his exact position to find the nudge of that little foot again. Gracie rubbed Josie's belly on one side, William patted her on the other, and the baby flipped and kicked.

She thought of the spiderweb again, and the doomed fly or bug that would finally send the web shaking. How the spider would crawl over, roll its prey in silk, then mount the knot of thread to pierce the insect's flesh. And that insect—trapped, paralyzed, alive. How much did it know? Would it be scared? At some point, she thought, closing her eyes and resting her head against the wall behind her, while Grace and William and Whoever-It-Was inside kept rubbing and pushing and kneading her, inside and out—at some point, you would have to get past the fear. If you were a smart bug, anyway. A smart bug would know enough to let go, to submit to the spider's need. A smart bug would see the wisdom in giving itself over to its sudden clarified purpose.

The thing was she doubted any bug was that smart.

The Nature of the Sun
by Jody Hobbs Hesler

Behind Mina, out the sliding glass doors off her sister Ruth's kitchen, crape myrtles blow bright pink blossoms into the wind, and lightning-bright gold finches dart from bird feeder to bird feeder in the backyard. Mina keeps her back to the colors and the sunshine, and tries to concentrate on her niece. That should be easy – Noreen is one of Mina's favorite people. But Mina's having one of her dark feelings, the kind that presses and presses inside her head as if it's about to burst out of her. The best she can do is lean over the counter to watch from time to time as seven-year-old Noreen fingers the puzzle piece fragments of goldfish and the haphazard aquamarine and midnight blue shapes of the water they swim in.

It's the first time Mina's sister has asked her to watch Noreen since the broken arm a month ago, and she wants everyone, including herself, to believe she can do a good job. Mina was pushing Noreen on the tire swing behind Grammy and Grampy O'Bannon's house when it happened. Mina had wound the tire swing rope super-tight, the way Noreen liked, and let it whap-whap-whap itself unwound. Maybe Mina had twisted it tighter than she had before, or maybe she'd looked away for a second too long, or maybe a funny breeze had interfered. Anyway, Noreen lost her grasp, her tiny body thudding to the ground.

At first, Mina had thought the worst part was the sound

Noreen's body made, or the way the fall knocked the breath out of her, but then she saw the bone poking gruesomely out of the arm Noreen had landed on. Afterward, all the grownups agreed that kids will fall and hurt themselves no matter how careful you are, and Ruth had never said anything out loud to suggest blame, but Mina feels responsible anyway. Every glimpse of the glaring white cast cuts to her heart.

Right now Ruth is out shopping for Noreen's brother's back-to-school clothes – she says it never quite works to clothes-shop with both of her kids at the same time. Mina suspects that if Ruth had anyone else to ask today, she wouldn't be here herself – a feeling she got from her sister's rigidly pursed lips as she reminded Mina one more time, "Be careful of her arm. She can't afford to hurt it again."

Maybe her sister would've said this to anyone, but Mina doesn't think so. Though Ruth never said anything out loud to blame Mina for the broken arm, she'd never said anything out loud to absolve her either, leaving a feeling of doubt between them. Now Mina can't help but picture that day differently – with someone else tending the tire swing, turning around in time to see Noreen beginning to lose her grip, in time to catch her, long before she hit the ground. No matter what anyone said or left unsaid, Mina never could seem to turn around in time for anything.

~ ~ ~

Lately, Noreen has done enough puzzles and colored in enough pictures with her clumsy left hand to last her a thousand summers of boredom, all while her brother and his friends have gone swimming and running through sprinklers and climbing trees. And her puzzle isn't any fun with no one helping. Noreen wants her aunt to think up something fun for them to do so she can leave the jumbles of orange fish to themselves.

Aunt Mina is twenty-three – too young to be a regular grownup and so much younger than her mother that most of the time she's really good at playing.

Whatever they decide to do, it'll have to be inside, though. Summer's a lousy time for a cast – the way it keeps Noreen from doing everything she likes and also itches, especially when she's outside and her arm sweats and bakes inside the plaster.

But she's excited to be starting second grade in a week and with such a trophy from her summer. Only her brother and his best friend have signed it yet, so it's still bright white with just the few broad black marks of their names. On her first day of school, she'll get all her friends to sign it.

"I bet I'll be the only kid with a cast," she boasts to Aunt Mina. "Or anyway, I bet none of the other casts are this big!" Noreen's cast goes almost to her shoulder.

It's one of those days Aunt Mina seems to have brought clouds with her, which isn't really fair because on days like that there's no chance at all that Aunt Mina will be the one to think of something for them to do. Just like the rest of the whole boring summer, Noreen will have to think up what to do all by herself. If she didn't have the cast, it would be easy. Her arm wouldn't crawl with sweat from the heat, and she could get soaking wet, so they'd go outside where they could race each other up and down the backyard or hunt for butterflies or wade in the pond.

But Noreen does have a cast, so she keeps talking. Sometimes, when she talks the exactly right amount, the sad look clears away from Aunt Mina's face and the laughing comes back. Noreen loves Aunt Mina's laugh – the way it bubbles up and out of her and puts a shine back into her eyes.

"At school," Noreen says, "they'll have to get me a helper, to write things down for me." She's right-handed, and that's the arm that's broken. "Just like last year, when this new kid showed up in our class? He had a helper."

"Did he, now?" Aunt Mina says her eyes fixed on something behind Noreen. Noreen turns her head to see what she's looking at, but all she sees is floor.

"Yeah, that kid with the helper? He almost drowned last summer, and something went wrong with his brain? His helper,

12

Miss Lewis? had hair all the way down to her butt. And she sat with him all day, just him and nobody else. They did something with sounds? Teaching him to make his sounds right all over again or something." Noreen nods her head, excited to think of getting a helper just like that.

But Aunt Mina's eyes widen and she says, "Oh God," just under her breath, so Noreen can see this wasn't the right story to tell to get her aunt to laugh again. Instead of laughing, Aunt Mina puts her coffee spoon down onto the counter, walks over to the kitchen sink, and pours the rest of her coffee down the drain. Her eyes still stare out to nowhere.

Noreen leaves her puzzle and pops up onto the sofa in the living room. It isn't nice for Aunt Mina to have a cloud day when Noreen is so bored and absolutely fed up from thinking of things to do all day long that are never the things she really wants to do, like swimming. Days when Noreen feels the way she thinks her aunt feels right now, Noreen's mother scolds her: "Don't be a pill," she might say. "Things only seem worse when you feel sorry for yourself."

But Noreen's mother isn't here, and Aunt Mina's too old for scolding anyway, so Noreen calls to her instead, "Come on over here. Let's play a game."

Aunt Mina lowers herself to the floor in front of the sofa where Noreen sticks her bare toes up into the air at the edge of the fuzzy, brown seat cushion. "Why are you sad?" Noreen asks. She flops onto her back on the sofa so her head is even with Aunt Mina's head, and her left hand twiddles a rope of her aunt's hair between her fingers. She loves Mina's wild frizzy ringlets, the flowery scent of her shampoo.

"What makes you think I'm sad?" Aunt Mina asks.

"I don't know. You are, though, right?"

~ ~ ~

Mina knows that grownups are supposed to help children with their feelings – not the other way around – but her niece's uncanny

13

sense of her always throws her off. She tucks her knees up to her chest and rests her chin on top of them. "Yeah," she says. "I guess I'm sad."

"How come?"

"I don't know, angel. Sometimes, I just wake up sad. I hope that never happens to you."

Her niece's hand comes to rest on Mina's shoulder. "I wish it wouldn't happen to you."

Then Noreen fidgets to life, bouncing the sofa cushions against Mina's shoulders. "I know! I have a game we can play." She hops to the floor, tilts a cushion on its side on the sofa, like a bed pillow, and pulls her aunt to standing. "Now, lie down," Noreen says.

Mina curls into the sofa, letting her eyes close. But Noreen's not finished. She darkens the room as best she can, using her left hand to tug the curtains closed behind the sofa and to turn off the living room light. "There," she says. "It's night time. Night, night, Aunt Mina."

"Night night, angel."

Noreen leaves the room. Mina can hear her, huddled in the hallway, waiting, giggling. Then she charges out, thrusting open the half of the curtains she can work with one hand. "Ta-da! Morning!" She dances into place beside the sofa, and leans over Mina. "Well, good morning, Aunt Mina," she says in a funny, fake voice. "I am the Sunshine, and it is morning now."

"Good morning, Sunshine," Mina says, and a smile begins to curve her lips. Look what magic Noreen can do – whisking away the darkness with a flick of her wrist.

"It is a new day now," Noreen continues in the Sunshine voice. "It is a good day. Today is a very good day."

"Is it?"

"It is, and now it's time to get up. Sit up and stretch now, okay?" The Sunshine voice slips back to Noreen's regular voice, but Mina's already sitting up and stretching, pretending to yawn.

"What a good sleep," Mina says. "Wow. What a nice Sunshine you are."

"Why, thank you," Noreen says. She talks with Mina for a while as the Sunshine, until Mina's back in the kitchen, dumping out the remaining pot of lukewarm coffee and starting a fresh one.

The aroma from the coffee begins to fill the room. The real sunshine shifts patches of tree shadows around the back yard, and everything is beautiful again. Mina turns toward the bright colors outside now and watches how the sunshine makes them even brighter.

When Noreen returns to the kitchen from her bedroom, her arms are burdened with books. A few of them slide to the floor in her wake because she can only steady the sprawling pile with her left hand. "Here, Mina," Noreen says, searching for a place for them to sit so she can empty her armload, "I'll read to you. I got all your favorite books."

For a few minutes, the love from the child in Mina's lap, the halting words of the stories she's reading, and, from outside, the perfect songs of the birds and the colors of springtime all drum the muddy nonsense from Mina's mind. Right here – this – is exactly what she knows how to do, and, at least for right now, she won't harm anyone at all. Forget that no amount of love will keep Mina's strange sadness from creeping back in and taking her over again, and remember instead that it doesn't hurt the sunshine to break through a cloud or to brighten every darkness it finds. That's just the nature of the sun.

So Mina allows herself to bask in Noreen's attention, listening as her niece reads all the books she's brought that have been read so many times to her. Whenever Noreen pauses to sound out the harder words, Mina's quick to nod and prompt her, believing in those moments that she's the one giving encouragement.

Inevitably, all over again, the white brightness of Noreen's cast catches the sunlight and cuts to Mina's heart; the noise of the birds outside begins to ring shrill in her ears; and the fuchsia of the crape myrtle blossoms becomes entirely too much to bear; and, as always, no amount of danger – real or imagined – can induce Mina to turn around in time to catch herself.

~ ~ ~

Noreen pretends not to notice when Aunt Mina goes back to staring at an empty space beyond her. She puts her books away in her room, returns to the card table where the many broken pieces of fish and water wait to be put together again, and wishes for a day when someone else would think of something fun to do with her.

Outside the backdoor, Noreen can see how hard the sun is shining today. She wonders, does it ever get tired from all the work it has to do? Noreen thinks it must.

Have You Seen Me?
by Kathy Lanzarotti

The woman on the phone is talking, but I don't believe a word. I shut my eyes and breathe deeply. Four counts in. Eight counts out. I open my eyes. The way the sun streams in on a day like today; the way its rays fire the facets on the crystals from the chandelier in the open foyer and speckle the upstairs wall behind me with rainbow stars, it's easy to forget that all is not right with the world.

"You're a psychic," I say as I focus on the light show.

"Well," she answers. "I'm actually more of a medium."

Medium. Sounds so much better than *quack*. She sounds about my age, maybe a little younger, but honestly, who can tell on the phone? Why do these women do this? Why don't they join the PTO? Sell Avon? Mary Kay? Something that doesn't harm anyone. I, for one, would much rather be driving around in one of those pink tinted Escalades than sitting on the phone in some crappy apartment harassing distraught mothers. Still, even though I know it's all lies, I can't allow myself to hang up.

"Alright, let's hear it." I know, I sound jaded. Irreverent. Just plain bitchy.

The woman is silent on the other end.

I sigh. I'm losing interest. Ava's little pug dog Cassandra, her fourth birthday present, waddles into the hallway. She grunts and snorts. Her flat nose hovers up and down the cuff of my pajama bottoms like a bee on a glass of lemonade. Cassandra knows what

17

happened to Ava. She looks up at me; her head moves right to left, so that her eyes, aimed east and west, can take in my whole face. She was there. She saw whoever it was that took my little girl. The only witness to my daughter's abduction can't say a word. I scoop her onto my lap and take a seat on the bottom step of the circular staircase.

"You there?" I'm mocking her. I can hear it in my voice. Casual. Apathetic. Glib.

"You don't believe me," the woman says.

"Hey!" I say. "You really are psychic!" I've heard all of this before. The psychics called a lot early on. Sometimes more than one a day. Wanting to tell me what happened to Ava. Who took her. They'd "see" a white box truck. A red pickup. A green Honda Civic. They'd tell me they "felt" her in the woods. In the snow. The river. Oblivious to what it was they were really saying to me. But then they tapered off. Lost interest. This is the first one in over a year. Maybe she's new. In training. Like a real estate agent. Start with the houses that have sat on the market a while. The ones with the outdated kitchens. Corian countertops. Mauve carpeting. Brass.

"I've spoken to her." Her voice is insistent, confident even. This doesn't move or inspire me, doesn't give me hope. They all say this. But just to be sure, I ask anyway, "You've seen Ava? You've actually spoken to her?"

She takes a deep breath and exhales the words. "Well, not physically, no."

"That's what I thought." I'm ready to hang up when she interrupts.

"Well, see, the way it works is, they contact me." She drags out the last word, like it's some irresistible treat that she's keeping from me. Like I'm just dying to hear more.

And I sort of am.

"They?"

She says nothing.

"You there?" Cassandra shifts with a grunt, sharp claws in my thigh, but it's okay. "Who's *they*?"

"Oh, I'm sorry," she specifies. "The lost."

The lost. Two years later. Still just lost. "I'm listening," I say.

"Ava says she loves you and misses you."

The tears surprise me still, the way they spring suddenly to soak my face. With them comes the grief, the misery and the contemplation of a three-martini breakfast.

Thanks, bitch.

"Mommy," the psychic says. "She says she misses mommy."

I'm trying to imagine this woman. I'm thinking mid-thirties, with shoulder length, dyed blonde hair, brushed back on the sides and over curled bangs. A sweatshirt from some sports team stretched over her large body. Several chins.

"Ava says she misses your goodnight kisses."

I'm imagining a special room in hell made up just for this woman. I'm thinking about the rack. Her limbs pulled loose in the sweatshirt like dolls' arms in the hands of overzealous children. The guillotine with a dull blade. Getting caught in her hair. Have to try again. Sorry.

"And she misses her daddy."

"I miss her daddy too," I say.

I'm pretty sure this was not the response she was expecting, but she bounces right back. "I understand how hard this all must be for you," she says.

"No," I say, thinking of Jack. "I don't think you do." Jack, those enormous, blue-green eyes. Ava's eyes. Eyes that change depending on what he's wearing: in green they darken to the color of an empty bottle of burgundy. In blues and purples, he's all pastels, his skin flushes pink, his eyes go clear blue. Jack with just a trace of Mid-Atlantic accent that slips out when he's tired, angry, or has had too many beers. Jack, over a decade ago, sauntering across a packed room, red plastic cup in his hand, at a party hosted by someone neither of us could ever remember. *Why don't you drop the stiff you're with and come with me?* Jack, kissing me hard, one hand open on my not yet swollen belly the day the pregnancy test turned pink.

19

Jack, red-faced hands tight on my shoulders, shaking me. Shaking me hard, but it's okay. *Why did you leave her? What in the world could be so important that you had to leave her?* Jack, pushing heavy suitcases into the trunk of his BMW. The car sagging under the weight. I watch the red taillights light up at the corner, the yellow turn-signal flashing. I watch the car until it disappears behind the trees.

"Ava's a beautiful girl," the woman says, shifting the conversation back into familiar territory.

"Yes," I say. "She is."

Of course, everyone knows Ava is a beautiful girl. Her kindergarten class picture was everywhere. The local news. The national news. *People* magazine "Every Parent's Nightmare: What Happened to Ava McAllan?". That crass blond Southern woman and the mannish lady with the Bell's palsy devoted entire segments to her on cable TV. I didn't think the class picture was her best. That isn't Ava to me. Her smile is a little off kilter. Her right eye is a little bit closed. I put her hair in pigtails, which she hates, and she cried like a baby when I turned those elastic cupcake bands. Once. Twice. Three times. She's dressed in her favorite blue jumper with the dog face: a furry pink tongue and brown ears. She used to kiss the dog before she put the jumper on. Little lips shut tight. She'd lean in with a loud "Mmmwah!" She'd look up at me with those big blue eyes and smile, curls bouncing lightly around her shoulders. That's my Ava.

"Ava told me all about her room," the woman says, and I can hear her smiling. "Winnie the Pooh and Piglet."

"Yes," I say. "Piglet is her favorite." On my lap Cassandra squeaks out a yawn. I can't resist adding, "But then I guess you knew that." In the mural up on Ava's bedroom wall Piglet bounces on a makeshift trampoline, a red blanket pulled taut by his friends. There is a happy smile on his upturned face. On Ava's bedroom wall even Eeyore doesn't look too gloomy. Not a care in the Hundred Acre Wood. A scene to suggest the sweetest of dreams for children in comfortable beds, dressed in footie pajamas after a good dinner and a bath with lavender scented bubbles. Children that didn't disappear from their front yards. Children that didn't leave one shoe, pink and purple with light-up hearts, in the middle of the road. Children safe at home. Stories with happy endings. Hell, at this point I'll take a story with any ending. Any ending at all.

And just in case you were wondering, it doesn't take a psychic to know about the mural. It was in the photo spread in *People*. They wanted to show Ava's room as it was when she disappeared. As it is now, actually—and ever shall be. They wanted a picture of me sitting with Cassandra on Ava's bed, surrounded by her abandoned dolls: Piglet, Dorie the fish and Sylvester the crab. All of us left behind.

I politely declined.

"She told me she was a princess for Halloween last year," the woman says brightly, like we're friends now.

"Nope," I say. I push the palms of my hands down the dog's back and come up with clumps of fur.

"Excuse me?"

"She wasn't a princess for Halloween last year."

"Oh," she says like she's legitimately shocked. She has to be the worst phony psychic ever. "She told me—"

"She didn't tell you anything, lady."

Silence.

"She was a princess the year before last for Halloween," I say. I gently lift Cassandra off my lap and stand up. "She wasn't anything last year, and do you know why?"

"N-no," the woman says softly.

"Come on! Of course you do! It was all over the news! The paper! The candlelight vigils? The teddy bears? Those sad little teddy bears. Bet whoever made those bears had a really different plan for them, don't you think? I'm thinking more along the lines of happy smiles and tender hugs. Not exactly. Come on, you saw it. The flowers that all died? The homemade cards that turned back to pulp in the rain?"

"Well—" she starts. But I'm not finished.

"The children's choir? All her little kindergarten friends singing "Amazing Grace"? Why is it always "Amazing Grace"? They're all in second grade, now. Learning their multiplication tables and how to write in cursive. But not Ava. No. Ava will always be the little girl in the flyer on the corkboard at the supermarket. Tacked to random lampposts. *Have you seen me?* No! Nobody has!" I take a deep breath: Four counts in. Eight counts out.

"But—"

"My daughter was not a princess for Halloween last year." My words are thick. Like a drunk trying to act sober.

"I think that maybe sh—"

"Be quiet," I snap. "She wasn't anything for Halloween last year. We don't know where she was last year. We don't know IF she was last year."

"Mrs. McAllan, I know this is a bad time—"

"Mrs. McAllan," I say. "Not according to the certificate of divorce."

That shuts her up.

"And it's always a bad time," I tell her. "There are no more good times here." When I say it, I'm reminded of how true it is. Jack and I, we were That Couple. A staple in the photo montage on the back of the Sunday paper. At the fundraiser for the symphony. The art museum. The Zoo. The same picture over and over again. The only variable was me. Hair swept up. Curled. Straight. In a pink dress. Black dress. Silver. The house with the coveted address in a suburb of quaint older homes. Nestled among oaks and elms. Neighbors close enough, but not too close. The beautiful little girl. Healthy and happy. More precious than all the rest.

I can hear her breathe in on the other end like she has something to say but has thought better of it.

"This is not a game, okay?" I say.

"I know that," she says.

"Again, I don't think you do." I look into the formal living room, never used except for company. I'm looking at the white couch that I picked out with Ava. Barely two and strapped into the rainbow-striped umbrella stroller. Her hair thick and glossy like puppy fur before it falls out. Ava in her green floral dress and barely used Stride Rite shoes, pristine soles with stars and circles of vivid red and blue. Ava with her stuffed Piglet doll in her round fist, his nose wet and misshapen by her tiny teeth.

"I—" she starts again.

"I had to get her dental records."

"If you'd let me—" she begins.

"I'm talking!" I place my BlackBerry directly in front of my mouth and speak very slowly. "Shut up and listen! You called me, remember?" I shift it back to my ear. Through the mahogany sidelights a squirrel takes three hops across the stoop and out of my line of vision. "It happened about six months after she was taken." I'm nodding my head so hard it hurts, but it's okay. The detective on the couch, hands clasped between his knees. Black wingtips on my peach and white oriental rug. They've found something. He tells me. And it's clear that by *something* he means *someone*. They don't know, he says. They just want to compare, he says. To rule out. His hands clench and unclench like time-lapsed flowers. Jack calmly shows him out, tells the detective he will get him whatever he needs. He wishes him goodnight and shuts the door. My head is down when I hear the first slam. I watch Jack punch the wall once. Twice. Three times. Watch the muscles in his arm flex and extend, flex and extend. Watch the blood smear on the cream-colored walls. He stops and sobs, his head against the wall. His face as red as the blood stain beneath his clenched fist.

Dental records. And all I can think about is the bag. The little purple satin drawstring bag. A gift from grandma, "To help out the Tooth Fairy." Ava's hair freshly washed, excited for once about going to bed. She drops in the lost tooth, and with one last smile proudly shows off what is no longer there. Little hands clap together as we carefully place the bag under her pillow. *Do you think she's pretty? Do you think she'll wear a beautiful dress?* Ava's eyes shut as I kiss her nose.

I wipe my eyes with the palm of my hand. "But guess what?"

I ask the psychic, and I don't wait for an answer. "It wasn't her." I swallow hard. "It was someone else's little girl." Outside, a red cardinal sits puffed on a branch like a signal flag. Black mask and yellow beak pointed straight at me. "Some other mother..." I trail off. Because what is there to say? Some other mother barely able to wrest herself from the unwashed sheets on her empty bed. Working the day on autopilot. Living to sleep. Because when you sleep you just might dream and when you dream you just might see your baby. Talk to her. Hug her. Instead I say, "But then, you probably knew that."

On the rug at my feet Cassandra sighs audibly, one bug eye aimed at the chandelier, one black ear flopped back pink onto her head.

"And you people, do you have a playbook or something?" I push my hair from my face. It needs to be washed. "What the hell is it with you people and Halloween costumes?" I pace a minute, my reflection in the floor sprouting from my feet, plaid pajamas and flat black hair even though it's two in the afternoon. "One of your, I don't know—colleagues, I guess? She was a lot better at this than you, by the way. She even mentioned the wand. The little gold wand with the glitter star tip that she had?" My hand is up in the air twisting to demonstrate. The tears are coming freely now. Ava loved that wand. She carried it around the house long after Halloween was over. She would bounce it lightly off Cassandra's blunt face. She told us that she was "granting wisses." Jack had joked that when he came home from work we'd have a golden retriever. To the psychic I say, "She really had me going with that one. Until someone gently reminded me that every Target, Wal-Mart and costume shop in the country sold those wands."

"MRS MCALLAN AVA SAYS IT'S YOUR TURN!"

This stops me. I reach out for the heavy oak table in the entryway. Was the tic-tac-toe board in the paper? Was it mentioned in the article in *People*? Could it have been? If you've ever been in a car with a flat tire, you've felt that thudding, hard bounce. The slight tilt. The loss of control. Shred that tire open at seventy-five miles

24

an hour and you'll know exactly how I'm feeling here in my foyer on this glorious Tuesday.

I walk slowly over to the stairs to sit. On the rug, Cassandra picks up her head. If you've ever owned a pug you know the look on their faces is pretty much always one of confusion or alarm. Right now, it's a little of both.

"How did you know—" I stop myself. I will not encourage this woman.

"She says you were *O* and she was *X*. She says she took her turn."

That was definitely not in *People* magazine. But, let's face it; it's not a huge creative leap.

"Why are you doing this to me?" I ask her.

On the driveway, Ava draws the game board: perpendicular lines from a thick cylinder of blue chalk pulled from a yellow box with smiling stick figures on it. She crosses the lines twice with pink chalk. So intent her tongue is visible between her lips. Cassandra beside her works her snout over the box, sneezes chalk dust and licks her nose with her long tongue. Ava shifts with a giggle; the little hearts on her shoes light up tachycardic, back and forth and back again. Cassandra crouches, ears forward, ready to pounce on them.

On the other end of the phone the psychic is shouting, "P Sherman 42 Wallaby Way Sydney! P Sherman 42 Wallaby Way Sydney! Ava keeps telling me P Sherman 42 Wallaby Way Sydney!"

Ava in her *Finding Nemo* t-shirt, a hand-me-down from her cousin. Ava loved that movie, especially Dorie the blue fish. She would walk quickly around the kitchen, a blanket over her shoulders, her arms flapping up and down at her sides. Cassandra at her heels, yapping and snorting, eyes on her moving arms. Ava would chant, "Just keep swimming, just keep swimming." Dorie the blue fish with the bad memory who remembered one very important thing: *P Sherman*—

"42 Wallaby Way Sydney! My God, she just keeps saying it!"

Before you think that this is significant, you need to know that the description of Ava's clothing was released to the public in the Amber Alert, along with her school picture.

"Please," I say. "Please stop." But I don't think she can hear me.

"She says you said you'd be right back—"

The moan that escapes stuns even me. At my feet Cassandra sits up and growls briefly.

"She says she waited."

I am rocking on the step. My eyes shut tight. Ava pushes her bronze curls off her face with the back of her hand, a smudge of blue chalk on her nose. She draws a big *X* in the center square. Rolls pink chalk to me. *You go now Mommy. You're 'O'.*

"I forgot the glasses." I say it quietly. "I forgot the white wine glasses."

"She says she did what you said."

"I had guests coming." My voice is weak. "I had potatoes in the oven," I say, despite how ridiculous it sounds. I cover my face with one hand. My eye sockets feel heavy and raw. But I can't cry anymore. My tear ducts have given up for now. *What in the world could be so important that you would leave her?* Potatoes baked with fennel and onion in heavy cream with gruyère cheese. Jack's favorite. Three of the partners and their wives were coming. I had salmon marinating in the refrigerator. "I brought the timer out with me."

Ava smiles. The silver timer with the black plastic face ticks off the minutes. I scrape an *O* into the upper right hand corner. I kiss the top of her head and breathe in cherry almond shampoo. *I'm gonna run inside for two seconds, Sweet Pea.* I get up and grab the timer, still ticking. *Take your turn.*

I'll be right back.

How long was I gone? When the timer went off I was in the dining room. The table dressed in a white cloth. Platinum rimmed dishes at each place setting, topped by silver-ringed napkins and flanked by sterling flatware. A large vase in the center tightly packed with fluffy white peonies. At the china cabinet, I lift out the teardrop shaped stemware. After lifting them to the light to check for spots, I place one at each setting, right where they belong, at the upper right-hand corner above the knife, just between the water goblet and the wide-bowled burgundy glass. Outside Cassandra barks and barks. But if you've ever owned a pug, you know that they bark at everything. Even a strong breeze. In the kitchen I push my hands into quilted oven mitts, pull open the heavy door and take out the potatoes. The gruyère has baked golden around the edges, and the kitchen fills with the licorice scent of roasted fennel. I realize that Cassandra is still barking. She hasn't stopped. I slide off the mitts and drop them on the floor on my way out.

"She says you shouldn't worry about her," the woman continues.

Outside on the driveway, the tic-tac-toe board is smudged. Two *X*s and one *O*. The pink chalk is crushed to powder, the blue stopped at the base of the drive. Cassandra marches back and forth, back and forth, her little beige body taut and tense. Her tiny head in the air. A long mournful howl bounces off the house and the trees and echoes back to me. Sounding the alarm. She stops howling and turns to me, unfocused eyes surprisingly on target. *And where the hell have you been?*

But no Ava.

"Ava says she doesn't want you to be sad."

In the street. The little pink shoe. The tiny red hearts light up here and there when I lift it off of the blacktop. This is all that is left of my little girl.

"Ava says it wasn't your fault."

Police cars, too many to count, clog the driveway. Officers across the street and down the block. Neighbors crowd at the curb. Dinner guests arrive, but never make it inside. The police officers politely send them home. Crime Scene. Do Not Enter. The phone has started to ring. Police in Ava's room. The basement. The garage. Standard procedure, according to Detective Lipsky, but Jack and I know what they are looking for. Signs of foul play. Of Death by Misadventure. Determining if we are victims or suburban monsters. We sit at the bare kitchen table and sort through recent photographs. The kindergarten picture. Ava in the pool, kept afloat by orange water wings, hair wet and straggled onto her shoulders, her eyes covered by blue goggles. Ava in her tutu, hair sprayed into a bun at the top of her head. She smiles wide and demonstrates a plié. Ava and Jack in Winnie the Pooh birthday hats. Her eyes wide and cheeks puffed as she blows out the candles on what no one ever dreamed would be her last birthday cake.

I shut my eyes and breathe: Four counts in. Eight counts out.

Ava says it wasn't your fault.

"Stop lying to me," I say.

Then I hang up the phone.

Rising from the Ashes
by Jennifer Gaskell

Mother's Day, 2011. I was at a free yoga class twenty minutes from my home, twenty minutes from my two daughters, a seven month old and a three and a half year old. At the end of class, I lay in relaxation pose, my body and mind relaxing into stillness and quiet. I hadn't felt this in days, to be honest, in months.

On my way home from the yoga class I realized something was wrong. Just two days before I had stood hiding in our bathroom sobbing uncontrollably as my little girls stared at me. Where had all the peace and stillness gone?

For months, mornings had been like this: frustration, tears, falling apart at not being able to get both my daughters out of the door on time. There was yelling, screaming and a rage from being overwhelmed. Why couldn't I do this? I only had two. I knew women who had more. My inner dialogue consisted of the same repeated word: failure.

The peace and stillness from Sivasana made me realize that something was wrong. It had been much too long since I hadn't felt like a jangle of nerves. Truthfully, I had not felt right since my daughter was born nearly seven months ago. I was existing, just surviving my life. I spent my days changing diapers, working full time, nursing, cleaning, and being with my family. I spent all my time outside of work with my husband and my daughters.

But I wasn't really there; it was just a ghost of me.

29

I hid behind a mask of forced smiles and feigned interest. Parenting had become nothing more than a long check-list of to-dos. Missed were the brilliant blue of my daughters' eyes that are so much like their dad's-- replaced by only shades of grey and clouds everywhere. Luckily, I knew enough to realize I needed help. I wanted more for my girls than the mom I was being.

My first step was to tell the person closest to me: my husband, Luke. Exploding into tears, I told him that I needed help. When I asked him if he thought I had been struggling, he replied "You have not been yourself since you became pregnant with our youngest. I never know what mood you are going to be in when I pick up the phone or walk through the door. I will support you in whatever you need to do to get better."

Based on that conversation we decided to call a therapist.

Without knowing what to say, my fingers shook as I dialed the number of a therapist I found. I left a message for her. My voice sounded more like a frightened child's than a grown woman. I heard myself leave my name and number. Sounding confused, I said, "This is Jennifer Gaskell. And something's wrong. I think it's anxiety. I want to be seen as soon as possible. I'm really struggling."

I felt some relief after that call, but I still felt scared. I couldn't do this alone. How could I explain and who would understand? The image of my sweet cousin's face floated before me. Not only is this cousin a close friend, but she is also a licensed social worker. I called her familiar number. When she answered, the words tumbled out of my mouth. "It's Jen. I'm not good. I think... I think I've got postpartum anxiety. I called and left a message for a therapist. I want to be seen right away." I had to reassure her, "I am not going to hurt myself or the girls, but I need help soon. Can you tell me what to say so I can get seen as soon as possible?" And with that confession, the floodgates opened, with all the anguish and anxiety I had been carrying alone for months. I burst into tears. Two days later, I was in my therapist's office, thanks in large part to the message that my cousin helped me to convey to my therapist.

My first therapy appointment, two years ago, was only one step of many – but it began my journey. Therapy along with medication controlled the overwhelming moments I experienced, but the most comfort I found was peer-to-peer support online. The Internet saved my life, and the first blog I logged on to was <u>Postpartum Progress</u> -- a site dedicated to providing mental health resources and support for women with postpartum issues. From there, I found a springboard for a live twitter chat online called <u>PPD chat</u> – where women from all over the world log on and find themselves in a safe place, where we can ask for understanding, acceptance, and community.

It was as if someone had handed me a tank of oxygen when I could no longer breathe on my own – I was no longer alone in my struggle. I had found a community of what we call, Warrior Mamas, women like me who work hard to survive and help others survive postpartum mood disorders.

I feel myself being reborn, like a phoenix refined from the ashes of my postpartum depression and anxiety. I want to share what I went through to let other moms know that they are not alone – that's why I started my blog, *tranquila mama*. I am not afraid to tell my story. I am thriving, strong enough to stretch beyond my comfort zone. I no longer just survive life; rather, I am living and loving my life, something I never thought I'd do again. I am recovering, and my journey has made me what I am today: the mother I want for my children.

Three and a half years ago, I was stuck, a struggling mess. And now, I am telling my story, hoping that someone out there, who needs to hear it, does.

And that they hear this – never give up hope.

The Prisoner
By Elizabeth Barrett Browning

I count the dismal time by months and years,
Since last I felt the green sward under foot,
And the great breath of all things summer-mute
Met mine upon my lips. Now earth appears
As strange to me as dreams of distant spheres
Or thoughts of Heaven we weep at. Nature's lute
Sounds on, behind this door so closely shut,
A strange, wild music to the prisoner's ears,
Dilated by the distance, till the brain
Grows dim with fancies which it feels too
While ever, with a visionary pain,
Past the precluded senses, sweep and shine
Streams, forests, glades, and many a golden train
Of sunlit hills transfigured to Divine.

Afternoon

"We must learn to regard people less in the light of what they do or omit to do, and more in the
light of what they suffer."

—Dietrich Bonhoeffer, *Letters and Papers from Prison*

Climbing Out
by Morgan Baker

The only thing I thought about at the ceramics studio was the ball of wet clay on the wheel in front of me. I didn't think about the changes in my family as I maneuvered the clay into a centered position and then pulled and opened it and looked into what would hopefully become a bowl.

I wasn't going to get depressed.

I was determined. I had fallen before, but this time I knew what to look for and what to avoid.

When I'd returned home in late August after dropping off my oldest daughter at college, the mornings were quiet like I had anticipated. Maggie didn't wake up, turn on her playlist on her laptop, carry it around the third floor, into the bathroom and back into her room at top volume. Only three people sat around the kitchen counter for meals. There weren't as many shoes and jackets in the front hall. The door to Maggie's room stayed shut. I didn't hear conversations or fights break out between sisters. Even our three dogs seemed less energetic.

With one less child at home, I knew I was going to have more free time and I had to figure out how to spend the time being dumped in my lap. Suddenly I was looking ahead with dread not just to the coming year with Maggie gone, but to the years coming when Ellie would leave as well.

The best way for me to deal with the impending loneliness was to be proactive. I needed to immerse myself in as many activities as I could so I'd have as little time as possible to think about Maggie or my new life and its changes.

Keeping busy seemed to work. The ceramics class distracted me, and a dog training class for the new puppy had kept me occupied one evening a week.

A rational observer would be able to spot many reasons why I shouldn't even be at risk for falling into a depression. I had two terrific daughters, a wonderful, funny husband, a nice house, a decent career as a part-time professor, and three challenging, but entertaining dogs. There was no reason for me to dislike myself or my life, but loss kicked irrational thoughts into action and depression doesn't listen to the rational side of an argument. It takes hold of the irrational and bangs it around so it is the only voice I can hear after a while. When it was active, I only heard how fat and lazy I was, how little money I brought home, how inefficient I was as a teacher and how pathetic I was as a mother and wife.

Few facts back up those assertions. In 2013, just before Ellie left for college I won a teaching award at Emerson College for excellence in the classroom, but when depression rears its ugly head, it can block out reality.

During previous depressive episodes, I had watched from above, appalled at what I was capable of doing to my kids and Matt, unable to stop being a bitch, unable to stop taking my anger out on myself, unable to apologize. If I could wish for anything – it would be for a rewind and a do-over. I would shake the Etch-A-Sketch clean.

Separating from those I loved wasn't one of the things I did gracefully. But when Maggie left, I was adamant with my therapist that I would be okay.

Teaching college students that year tested me. I started to project. My own children had always been younger than my students. Now, however, Maggie had caught up and when I looked into my classroom, I saw lots of Maggies. When students talked about their weekend activities – the parties they attended and the drinking they did, I wondered what Maggie was doing. If they wrote about missing their families or not missing their families, I saw Maggie in their essays. When I witnessed how stressed and tired my students were as the semester wore on, I worried about Maggie and her workload.

We visited Maggie a lot in September and October to watch her play goalie on the Vassar field hockey team. I, sort of, got used to saying good-bye to her at the end of the weekends. We developed a rhythm those months, but when October ended my mood started to shift, though I didn't realize this then. Plus turning the clock back at the end of October always marked a change in my state of mind, when the days were shorter and darker, I always did better with sunlight.

The only contact I had with Maggie after that was through Facebook and the phone calls she made as she walked between buildings on campus. As with many of her fellow students, the calls came randomly and ended abruptly when she reached her destination.

Every time I signed on to Facebook, sitting at my desk tucked away behind the TV room in my home office where no one could see me, I felt like a teenager with a crush, immediately checking to see if she was on. When I saw the green circle next to her name, my heart beat a little faster. If the circle didn't show up, I was a little down. I rarely engaged her in conversation. I just liked knowing she was there. I was obsessed. I missed her and our old family.

Maggie came home at Thanksgiving. She was happy to see and play with the dogs. She slept and did a little homework. I followed her around like one of the dogs and when she left at the end of the long weekend, I returned to the classroom, and I saw a dazed look on my students' faces – the same look I thought Maggie probably had on hers. It said, "Oh no, I didn't get as much work done as I should have and now it's crunch time until the end of the semester."

The Christmas madness – before, during and even after – helped me continue to ignore the signs that I was slipping into a depression. I tried hard to keep them hidden under my bed with the out-of-season linens. I didn't want anyone to know how bad I felt.

I hated feeling out of control, like I didn't own my body or my emotions. I looked at my half-finished quilts, including one for Maggie, and I couldn't go near them. Every time I thought of Maggie at school, I broke down, mostly in my office behind closed doors where no one could see me.

I excelled at sleeping, crying and berating myself. I was not kind to myself. I wouldn't want me for a friend.

I trudged through each day like a piece of flypaper. Flies collected on my body, sticking to me, slowing me down even more, hiding the real me.

I wanted to sleep, I didn't want to see my friends. I was scared I might start to cry. I was on edge, as though a crack was running through me and I would break into many pieces.

After Christmas, with Maggie home once more, my therapist again suggested the idea of anti-depressants. She thought they would keep me from slipping further into the valley I was clearly falling into. I kept telling her and myself I could talk and work myself out of the funk I was in. If I just stayed busy with more pottery, dog classes, and teaching, I would be fine.

But I wasn't being honest. With her or me.

Even the dogs couldn't make me smile.

I didn't want to admit to anyone how weak and helpless I felt. I was scared a lot of the time, anxious, shaky, unsure of myself and sad. I wasn't sure what there was in my life to be happy about. Loss loomed wherever I looked.

I didn't want to be on medication. I didn't like the side effects it inevitably brought with it – dry mouth, low sex drive, weight gain, sleepiness – and I didn't like thinking that this dark cloud in my head could only be controlled by artificial means. What did that say about me, and my strength of character that I couldn't control it alone?

I became even shakier and started crying even more. Maggie

and her long-term boyfriend Jay tried to lighten my mood by taking bets on how often I would cry each day – but first they had to agree on a definition. Did welling up count? Or did tears have to fall?

In the kitchen, making cookies, a favorite pastime of mine, I would start to cry thinking of Maggie returning to school after Winter Break.

"Look, she's crying again," Maggie might say.

"Any tears?" Jay would ask. "I am not," I'd argue as I turned back to the sink.

For a moment, their contest would make me smile.

No matter how many friends told me that you never really lose your children, that you're always a parent, I knew that Maggie had left home for good. Even if she were to come back to "live" with us, it would only be as a visitor. Our family unit was in transition and I didn't do transitions well.

It was easy to miss what was behind me – the Saturday soccer games and Sunday morning church outings – I could see, feel, taste and smell them. I didn't know what was ahead. I couldn't see it and I was scared of the unknown. I looked at young moms with their babies or toddlers going for walks and I was jealous, but at the same time, I thought evil thoughts – "Just wait; those sweet little children are going to leave you too."

No matter how much awareness there is about depression and mental health in general, I felt the stigma associated with it, perhaps because I grew up hearing the mantra "pull yourself up by your bootstraps" when the going got tough, or perhaps because people are more comfortable talking about their sore throats than their mental health issues.

I didn't like to think of myself as someone with the big D. I didn't like to think of how my illness and consequently, my behavior, affected Matt, Maggie, and Ellie. I hated the TV ads that emphasized how depression affected those around the depressed person. I wanted to yell at the voice-overs and tell them to shut up.

Eventually, my therapist convinced me to try Nortrptyline,

an older anti-depressant from the tricyclic family. It was stronger with stronger side effects, but she was hopeful it would pull me out of the deep despair I had slipped into.

I wish I had woken up one morning as a changed person – one of those perky, always upbeat, look-on-the-bright-side-of-life people who always have something positive to say about everything. But that didn't happen.

Climbing out of my depression wasn't easy or fun. It took weeks for the meds to kick in. It was frustrating as hell waiting. While I wondered if they would ever do their job or if it was all just a big waste of time and effort, I felt like crap.

After two weeks, I had an easier time getting through the days. Teaching, which had always been an escape for me, wasn't as energy draining except for the incredible dry mouth that left my lips smacking together as I lectured the class. I didn't cry all the time and by Week Three, I was really functioning pretty well. I didn't have to talk myself into leaving the house. I could just walk out the door.

While the pills didn't change who I was, they made it easier to be me. I accepted the changes in my family more and focused on how I could adapt to those changes.

Climbing out of a depression is slow – it's a few steps forward and then a quick slide backwards, like in the movie *Homeward Bound*, when Shadow, the old dog, falls into a hole and tries to climb out of it, as he, Chance (the younger dog) and Sassy the cat make their way home after being separated from their humans. Shadow keeps slipping backwards and tells his buddies to go on without him. But with a cheering section above the hole, Shadow keeps trying and after a few false starts, he gets out.

With Matt, Maggie and Ellie, and my friends rooting for me, I kept at it, and over time got out of the hole. Matt said he knew when I was back and glad to have me back. Perhaps he recognized the real me when I stopped asking him every five minutes if he was upset he married me.

Perhaps he recognized me when I started laughing again,

something I generally love to do, but when depressed don't do often. Not much is funny then. But I laughed. I even laughed at the thought of Matt and me alone together after Ellie would leave us. There were times, when I thought, "Oh my God, really?" What would we talk about? What would we do? Then were the times when I thought of the dinners out, the movies and the trips and I thought, "Wow, this might be okay."

Neurological New Year's Logic
by Litsa Dremousis

As I occasionally do in crises, I'm counting on my bountiful rack to provide a distraction. I'm wearing a plunging v-neck white tee shirt, hoping my chest draws focus from the dark bags under my eyes and my unwashed curly hair spiraling out from under its sky blue knit cap.

It's late May and Seattle is unseasonably warm. My neighborhood sidewalks are crowded and when two passing guys stare way too long, I realize my left sleeve is now draped halfway down my bicep, leaving much breast and bra exposed. I look like an insomniac hipster prostitute.

Sometimes, I am the worst feminist ever.

I'm headed to the pharmacy and continue walking undeterred. Or maybe, beyond caring. I've slept less than ten hours over the past five nights and objects in my peripheral vision are starting to liquify. Despite the heat, my teeth have been chattering since morning. At the best of times, I often need a cane or crutches to walk (I've had CFIDS, similar to MS, for twenty-two years), but right now, the crutches are all that prevent a skull-shattering face plant. I wrote poetry most of the night before, committing my swirl of racing thoughts to the page. I can't drive, obviously, and didn't cab it because I'm hoping the long walk will help finally propel me to sleep.

My mind is a movie screen and a cruel trickster is running the projector, bombarding me with horrible images and echoes. A voice that sounds disturbingly reasonable, even soothing, keeps noting how peaceful things could be if I killed myself. Such episodes–I call them "chemical storms"–began when I was twelve and have returned throughout my life, but only a handful of loved ones and clinicians know. This is by far one of the worst and I'm scared like an animal that eluded the trap, only to find itself in a cage.

How the hell did I get here again?

*

"You're just like your mother! Be careful or this could happen to you!" Dad yelled as we drove to retrieve Mom's car from the psych ward she'd unexpectedly checked herself into that morning.

"He's right, Litz. You don't want to end up there," my brother Gus added from the passenger side of our wood-paneled Mercury Zephyr station wagon.

I sat in the back middle seat and remained still, as if epoxied to the burgundy vinyl. I'm naturally shy but dodge it with reflexive verbosity. This was a rare instance in which I was stunned speechless.

"You're so much alike! You get depressed! You cry!" Dad continued. On the list of things you might want to hear from your dad while on the way to the psych ward where your mom was newly harbored, this ranked slightly above "Those bangs will never work on you" and a notch below "You're actually Rosemary's Baby."

It was the start of my sophomore year at the University of Washington and Seattle's autumn light beamed through the car windows. Gus had just begun his senior year of high school and proudly wore his letterman's jacket. If you discounted the circumstances, it was a lovely pastoral afternoon. But Dad kept warning of my eventual mental collapse and Gus kept agreeing with him and, with the best of intentions, they rendered the already frightening events positively terrifying.

Because we knew Mom's depression had flooded the house again, like a mutinous river or blood gushing from the elevator in

43

"The Shining". But its strength this time had caught us off guard. All four of us are Greek-American and prone to epic emotions (Greeks are the original dramatists, after all), but even compared to Dad, Gus, and me, Mom's highs were far higher and her lows alarmingly cavernous. Or I'd always thought so, anyway. Now, like ringside judges, Dad and Gus were declaring Mom and me a draw in the Bout of Big Feelings.

Renowned depressive and eventual suicide Ernest Hemingway concluded at the end of his life, "Happiness in intelligent people is the rarest thing I know" and in some ways, Mom exemplified his theory. A brilliant attorney and bibliophile, she both examined the big picture and noticed the smallest detail and that, of course, can lead to upheaval.

But when she was happy, her warmth radiated like the sun. She hosted rollicking Sunday dinners for our extended clan and at the holidays, always welcomed friends who had nowhere else to go, even providing chocolate Santa-filled stockings at Christmas. When Gus and I were kids, she taught us to roller-skate and read us everything from Beatrix Potter to *Newsweek*. In non-psych ward related matters, being compared to Mom was a great thing.

"I never want to see you in a place like this!" Dad kept repeating like the world's worst wind-up toy as we drove into the hospital parking lot, his Greek accent thickening as it did during times of stress.

"It's not like I'm planning on it, Dad!" I finally responded, exasperated. "Now does anyone actually know where Mom left her car?" I asked, trying to focus on matters at hand.

*

When I get to the front of the line, I explain to the pharmacist that my doctor has phoned in a rush order for Valium and for Zoloft. My shirt slides again and I'm wondering why I thought cleavage would help matters. Like, hey, I'm picking up two different rush-ordered mind meds, but don't I look fertile? The pharmacist is matter-of-fact as he retrieves my order and I remind myself he sees a cornucopia of human behavior on any given day. I'm outwardly lucid, after all, and am able to calmly pay and sign my name.

As I turn to exit, "Back on the Zoloft again!" wafts through my head to the tune of "Back in the Saddle."

I might be depressed, but can still ferret out a punch line and find this weirdly reassuring. Then I recall all the times in my twenties I consciously and subconsciously blamed Mom for her depression and am reminded I can be a cruel idiot.

*

By genes and by circumstance, I was as likely to escape major recurring depression as a bowl-roaster is to forego Doritos. Not only did depression profoundly impact Mom until she received proper treatment, but it also afflicted her similarly brilliant and dynamic parents. And CFIDS, of course, is degenerative, incurable and limits my mobility, often rendering me unable to leave the house for more than an hour or so. Four years ago, my partner died when I was forty-two. For good measure, I'm a writer. And a woman. (All research shows writers have a high rate of depression even compared to other artists and women are more prone to depression than are men.) If a scientist were to create a depressive in a lab, a sort of super-bummed out Frankenstein's monster, she would resemble me, though maybe with a less awesome rack. (Again, I'm going off statistics here.)

So what in fucking hell was I doing off my Zoloft?

Well, two years ago, the dose I was on stopped working. Instead of asking my doctor to adjust the dose or to switch to a new anti-depressant, I decided to taper off it. I was still deep in the grieving process and–this really did make perfect sense at the time–I thought nothing short of ether would do any good, so the hell with it. I'd give my liver a break and let my mind fly solo for a while. Also, I present atypically: while many depressives sleep more and do less, I tend to overcompensate, both in an attempt to outrun the awfulness and to throw everyone off the scent. As such, I publish frequently, have never missed a deadline and don't leave the house without an impeccable swath of lipstick. As I told my former shrink, "You'll always see me dressed up and I'll sound articulate and funny and it won't mean a goddamned thing." The grim apotheosis: one of the times I called the Crisis Clinic, the volunteer concluded dismissively, "You sound totally fine." And then she hung up.

But what happened in May has changed me. I wrote a long missive to two of my best friends and confessed how many times I've narrowly averted disaster. I gave them explicit permission to inquire whether or not I'm sticking to the Zoloft. And because they love me, they do. Each periodically checks in, not in a condescending way, but in a manner that shows they understand depression. They know that when I say part of me has wanted to die, I'm not being a dick. And they know bumper-sticker platitudes are worthless. My namesake died under Nazi occupation, for god's sake: I know so much of my life is great and that I have an easier hand than most of our planet's inhabitants. But when the death voice wails like an air raid siren, perspective falls victim to the noise.

Depression, by definition, makes those of us who live with it feel incredible guilt. If we're honest, we might worry our loved ones. But if we stay quiet, we're risking our lives.

I will undoubtedly contend with further depressive episodes. And the CFIDS will continue to attack my body and, no matter what, my best friend will remain a wad of ashes in a titanium box.

But I really don't want to die.

So here's to 2014.

You guys aren't getting rid of me that easily.

The Weight of the World
by Liam Hogan

It started with a suicide: mine. Failed, of course. This isn't one of those stories told by someone who turns out to be dead.

You probably want to know why I tried to end it all. But that isn't what this tale is about. There wasn't a solid reason for my actions, no smoking gun, if you will, no single straw that broke the camel's back. If you insist on a reason, the best I can give is this: in the end, the balance of pluses and minuses just seemed to weigh down too heavily on the debit side, and for a moment--and a moment is all it takes--the easiest solution seemed to be to close my account.

I even managed to make a mess of that and in my misery sat in the cold and damp, lost deep within my black thoughts, long after the moment had passed.

"Budge up!"

The booming voice coming out of the dense night fog almost made me jump, which would not have ended well, given my legs were sticking out over the edge of the bridge. I looked up at the stocky figure that had loomed unnoticed into view. "Are you... a cop?" I asked, half-fearful, half-hoping.

He squatted down by my side; a strange stance, uncomfortable looking, but somehow immensely powerful: a weightlifter ready for the clean and jerk.

"No, I'm not," he said, quieter now, but still shockingly loud after the lonely hours of silence. "I don't think they know you're here. I don't think *anyone* knows you're here, except for you, and for me."

"And you are?" I asked, shivering a little.

He laughed, a ripple of a laugh, subdued and self-deprecating. The bridge seemed to rumble in response. "Oh, you know me," he said. "Even if they don't teach the classics any more, or tell tales of gods and heroes, you'll still have seen my statue, or at least, a picture of my statue. You know the one: a mighty globe held aloft between my bowed shoulders, my head bent under the weight, one hand in the East, and one in the West. And you might have heard of the mountain range named after me, though I'll warrant you've never seen it in person."

My mind chewed through his riddle. "Atlas?" I guessed.

"The one and only." He held out a muscular hand. I hesitated for a moment and then rubbed the grit from my palm before warily reaching up. I was awfully glad he didn't try to exert any pressure, I had the feeling my hand would have been crushed like an empty eggshell.

"And you are?" he asked, not yet releasing my trapped hand.

"Jacson Grut," I admitted.

He gave the most imperceptible of nods. "An unfortunate name."

I shrugged. What was there to say?

"You don't look much like your statue," I pointed out, after a moment's awkward silence.

"I guess not," Atlas replied. "I've seen them all you know, professional curiosity. Three thousand years and hundreds upon hundreds of artists; you would have thought that by now one of them might have managed a faithful representation, merely by dumb luck. Not that it really matters, not when you're trying to capture an idea."

Great, I thought. Perched precariously on the edge of a bridge, cold, damp and hungry, and I seem to have attracted the only other nutter out tonight.

"If you're Atlas," I said, "Aren't you supposed to be holding the Earth up?"

He gave me a baleful look. "And what would I stand on to do that? My burden is the sky, Mr Grut. Rather a difficult thing to represent in stone, the sky, so the early artists showed it as the celestial sphere, until some idiot mistook that for the terrestrial globe."

I looked at him, but said nothing.

"Let me ask you a question. Where does the sky meet the earth?"

I thought for a moment. "At the horizon?"

"Ever been there?" he snapped back.

I thought again, more carefully this time. "Everywhere," I said with confidence. "Gaseous molecules impinging on solid ground or liquid seas, bound to the Earth by simple gravity."

"Ah, so you're a rational man." His teeth, as solid and square as the rest of him, glinted in the yellow glow of the nearest streetlight. "Curious, then, that your first answer betrays millennia of human superstition. Superstition born out of a very real fear. There are so many ways the world might end that you've forgotten one of the oldest: the sky falling down upon your heads."

"But that's just a nursery tale," I protested. "The sky can't fall down, any more than you can hold it up."

"Can I not? My burden is not strictly the weight, Mr Grut, it is one of belief, an undervalued and much maligned currency in your modern age. And yet... tell me, what do you think will happen if you were to let go of that pillar, edge forward an inch or two, and slip over the side into the waiting fog? Do you think, because you cannot see the ground, that you will fall forever? Or perhaps that the cloud will softly close over you, gently washing away your woes and your worries as it claims your unwanted life?"

I opened and then shut my mouth, uncertain how to reply, uncertain why I had been sitting there for so very long as London retreated into unfamiliar silence at my back.

"Or does your rational mind tell you that the fog is immaterial-

-mere gaseous molecules--and your twenty-five foot drop will end less than two seconds after it begins with your body smashing against the concrete pier, your bones breaking, your organs crushed by the rapid deceleration, your body wracked with pain as you tumble to the mud and gravel below--because despite what you might think, you are not over the river, not quite, not here, not now--leaving you drifting in and out of consciousness, until finally high tide finishes the job, filling your remaining lung with cold, brackish water, your last burst of strength to plead to the heavens for help, or at least a swift release from a slow and agonising death?"

I gaped at him and felt my head swim with a sudden bout of vertigo.

"Woah there!" Atlas said, and pressed his hand across my chest. "Don't you go fainting on me! Just how long have you been sitting here?"

"About three hours," I admitted, though this was, at best, a guess, as both my watch and my mobile phone had been dropped into the shrouded abyss some time back.

"Hmm. Let me guess. Life is terrible, right? A string of failed relationships, your job sucking the very life out of you, nothing at all left to live for?"

I nodded, feeling a tear come to my eye.

"Feels like the weight of the world is on your shoulders?"

I started to nod again, and then looked up into his grinning face, and sheepishly smiled in response.

"Would you like to feel it, for comparison? The weight of the sky of course, not the world. And not the full weight either; only one human could ever manage that and he was semi-divine. About a thousandth should do it."

"Well..." I said, not entirely sure what he was asking me to do.

"Come!" he cajoled. "What's the worst that can happen? Surely nothing as bad as you were already contemplating?"

Put like that, I supposed not. "Then... okay."

"Good. But not here," he said, rising from his crouched position.

"You'll need your balance and it's definitely best if you stand well away from the edge. Up you get."

And so there I was, in the middle of the eerily quiet bridge, still wondering if this was a trick, some complicated Good Samaritan technique to coax would-be jumpers away from ledges and dangerous parapets, as Atlas manoeuvred my legs and arms into position. "Ready?" he asked.

I nodded once and would have done so again, but at that moment something slammed into my head and my shoulders. My legs buckled and my back arched under the crushing weight, and, with the wind knocked out of me, I looked up to see Atlas gently twisting his head from side to side and rolling his shoulders. With a series of crunches and sharp clicks, he stood erect and the weight was gone. For a blissful moment I felt as if I might float off into the fog.

"That... that was the weight of the world?" I gasped.

"The sky," he corrected patiently, pleasantly. "And only a fraction, though even that would have been enough to crush a superstitious man, Mr Grut. If you actually believed the sky needed supporting, you would have been flattened like a bug beneath a steamroller."

"How... how can you stand it?"

"I'm a Titan," he said. "It's what I do."

He paused, his brow furrowed. "Not that you make my task easy, with your skyscrapers and aeroplanes! You blur the lines between heaven and earth and if I was to lose concentration for even a moment, everything would come crashing down. It is especially difficult on nights like this, when the fog lies so heavy that it takes all my strength to force the sky to stay its course." Atlas said. "One of these days, perhaps I'll find an entirely rational man, who will agree to take my burden from me, and who won't even notice he is carrying it."

"And then?" I asked, rubbing the sore muscles on my shoulders, feeling the knots, feeling the warmth that comes with an intense gym session.

Atlas laughed. "And then I'll go on holiday. Or perhaps there will no longer be a need for me and I'll simply cease to be. But I've never met such a man yet and somehow I doubt I ever will.

"Well Mr Grut, a gentle breeze precedes the dawn and the fog is thinning. Soon, they'll reopen the bridge, and people will carry on, oblivious to the extreme danger the world was in tonight, is in every night. Time for me to go. One final question though; do you think your life would be bearable, if you had the perfect job, a flat you wanted to go home to, the ideal girlfriend?"

I shrugged. It seemed a cruel question, being so divorced from my reality.

"And what IS your perfect job? Who IS your ideal girlfriend?" Atlas asked, pointedly.

I stood there a moment in silence.

Atlas sighed. "Your problem, Mr Grut, quite apart from the name, is that your dreams are no more substantial than this fog. Go home, get some sleep, and dream big. You never know your luck in this wonderful world."

And then he walked into the swirling fog, vanishing from view. I looked after him, feeling tired: sleepy, rather than weary. I was alone again, but I no longer felt any desire to be anywhere near that deserted bridge, or the dark river that gurgled below.

The policeman seemed surprised to see me as I stepped between the flashing beacons at the barricade on the north side of the bridge. "They've opened up the other side," I said, to allay any suspicion he might have.

"Ah... thanks," he said, between stifled yawns. "Nobody tells me..." He hesitated. "Are you alright, Sir?"

I must have looked a fright, what with my rumpled sweat-stained shirt, my damp matted hair, and, no doubt, my blood-shot eyes. But I felt better than I had in ages. Like, really ages. Years. I wondered if, when Atlas had taken his immense burden back, he'd taken some of mine with it. Or perhaps was it just that having closed off one avenue--the quick and not-quite-as-easy-as-I'd-thought final escape--I knew then that I would have to go on, to persevere. That I would have to make the most of the little I had. Starting today.

"Never better, Officer," I said, as I walked on by. "Never better."

Fighting the Backbeat
by Pam Parker

For the most part, I can put on a good face -- smile and greet the world with sincerity and gratitude. I live a blessed life. But, there's a backbeat playing in my mind, a steady thrum pulsing behind the meetings, the phone calls, the visits.

My son said he wants to kill himself.

With these words, my attention and focus for my work -- my writing -- crumble like a stack of blocks kicked over by a three year old. The blocks lie scattered over my living room carpet with to do items scrawled on each one – finish seventh revision of novel, update blog, submit applications to residencies, finish and submit short story, update idea log. A blanket seems to cover the blocks and I tiptoe around, unable to uncover them and consider them, one at a time.

You see, my son said he wants to kill himself.

Mental illness has visited my family before, and my husband's family. It's become a frequent visitor – we've had suicides, bipolar disorder, clinical depression, and alcoholism. We also have a generous dose of attention deficit issues throughout the family, which can be a blessing for creative types, but obviously has its own challenges. All these issues have scratched their way into our lives.

Sure, there are treatments. There is hope. All the family members with the challenges I've listed live lives in a relatively comfortable zone – able to afford a roof over their heads (or, be helped by family to do so), food in their cupboards, transportation, and for most, a job.

My son has been trying for over a year to get a job. Most of his applications have fallen into the black hole of non-response land. He's had four interviews in those fourteen long months, followed again, by nothing. He's twenty-one going on seventeen and at times, thankfully, he is happy. His safe place is the stage. He recently landed the lead role in a local theater production. While he's in a show, he may still be unemployed, but he has a purpose. For me, this quiets the suicide thrum for a while. The backbeat is there, but softer. The volume will increase as his show progresses toward its inevitable close, especially if he hasn't found his next part.

Maybe my son won't want to kill himself. Maybe it's not my fault.

I don't wallow often in "what did I do wrong" land, but I do fret. The weight of worries is visible on my stomach, hips and thighs. I spend my days exploring residential therapeutic programs for him, trying to motivate him to complete another application that is likely to disappear in the ether, talking to my therapist, checking if he's made an appointment with his therapist – and all the while, I try to keep smiling, keep believing, keep showing a happy face, because I have to believe that my son will make it past the desire to kill himself.

I did.

This piece aired as an essay on "Lake Effect," a program on WUWM FM, Milwaukee Public Radio in 2014. Thankfully, the parties involved have moved past this moment in time.

The Guests that Wouldn't Leave
by Mel Miskimen

The Doom and Gloom twins always showed up uninvited and unannounced. I tried ignoring them, pretending I wasn't home. I'd turn off the lights. Crawl back into bed, pull the covers over my head, but they kept ringing my mental door bell, like a pair of persistent Jehovah's Witnesses who would not be satisfied with my, "Yes, yes, yes. Sure. Jesus Christ? Uh huh. Yeah. I've heard of Him. Just leave the literature. Thank you, buh bye."

They insisted on coming in. Making themselves comfortable. Would it have been asking too much for them to make their beds? Cook dinner? Put on pants? They would leave after they trashed my psyche like teenagers at a parent-less house party, tp'd my self-worth and spilled beer all over whatever was left of my self-esteem upholstery. How was I going to keep them from coming back?

A change in address didn't help. They still managed to track me down and let themselves in.

He was cardigan-d. Bearded. A hippie Mr. Rogers. He had pulled the short straw at the student health services when I went in for a twenty-five year, 40,000 mile, I-don't-know-what-I'm-doing-with-my-life tune up.

"Have you *not* heard of Catholic Guilt?" he said.

"It's a *thing*? Seriously?"

I left, re-aligned, with new tread, the sludge cleared out of my carburetor.

The twins found me after I gave birth. I wondered why I wasn't feeling like my friends who had fallen in love with their newborns before the cord was clamped and cut. I loved my child, but I wasn't *in love* with her.

They didn't help around the house. They wouldn't lift a finger. I would have appreciated a hint as to how long they planned on staying, because I had a lot of shit to do, and it wasn't getting done. I seem to recall them taking a brief respite after the six week well-baby checkup. Maybe the amitriptyline had something to do with it, I don't know, because I didn't care. About anything. And, I wasn't worried. About not caring. About anything. Which set me up nicely for a return to work, "Um, you know your shirt is on inside out and backwards?" No, I did not.

Maybe I had to learn to live with them. Annoying roommates. Fine. I would soldier on. I'd get up in the morning, brush my teeth and put on my brave face, layered underneath my faux-enthusiastic face, on top of my keeping-it-together face, trying to blend all perfectly and smoothly. Was that me in the mirror or Joan Crawford from Mommy Dearest? I needed a makeover.

Her office was very Zen. A table-top tranquility fountain gurgled. A potted bamboo plant stood in the serenity corner. I felt neither tranquil, nor serene. She was petite. Asian. Her long, dark hair was done up with a chop stick. Cliché? Her heavily starched lab coat crinkled as she took her seat on the chair. I hated this part. How would she begin her line of questioning?

How can I help?

What brings you here?

What's going on?

I was not prepared for "You're not thinking right! You don't think in reality! You want life to be like in a movie!" Was scolding a new technique? Who didn't want their life to be a movie starring Diane Keaton? She said I needed to make another appointment, which I did, but cancelled. The receptionist wanted to know why. I could have said something about a family emergency, but I figured the Doctor may benefit from constructive criticism.

"Oh . . . that's just her way. She cares about her patients."

"But she cares too loudly."

Therapy was serious stuff. But, there were times when I'd be talking and I'd see the therapist giggling. My Cuban Missile Crisis story? It killed.

"So, there I was, seven years old, getting under my desk, covering my head with my Flintstones lunch box–"

My history of family depression got a few spit takes.

"I think my Grandma was depressed. She used to sob quietly, but loud enough for everyone to hear, 'I'll be dead next Christmas, and then you'll be sorry,' and guess what? She was right. She died on Christmas Eve. But, no one was sorry."

On one of my last go-rounds on the therapy carousel, I got this:

"It's so hard to get out of bed, I mean, I just feel so worthless–"

He looked inside a file cabinet, "Uh Huh."

"–and I've got no energy for anything–"

"Uh huh." He rifled through a stack of file folders on a table.

"–I feel, like 'why even bother?'"

He sat down at his desk. Opened the file folder, "Well . . . your tests results show me that you are *not* pregnant. Is that good news?"

"It would be if I had *had* any tests."

I was done. Therapy nil. Doom and Gloom? Winning. I'd have to do the best I could, do the depression limbo – set the bar low, lower, really, really low. But, what the hell? Life for me, sucked. Did I think about ending it? I'd be a liar if I said I hadn't. Yeah, I thought about suicide. But, seriously? I hadn't the energy. And, then . . . there was the guilt factor about who would clean up the mess?

I trudged through the endless days of emotional winter, living in an Ingmar Bergman film. Going to bed at seven. Getting up to make the kids their lunches, get them to school, then 'napping,' getting up in time for the after school pickups, dinners and back to bed. I had a schedule. That seemed normal. Normal-ish.

Nothing like a terrorist attack to rekindle old Cuban Missile Crisis fears.

9-11 sent me over the edge. Was it the other shoe dropping,

the one that Sister Gregory had warned me about back in 1962? Or . . . was it one of a new pair? I was in the middle of duct-taping plastic to the windows, when my fifteen year old daughter said, "Um, Mom? I think you need to call this number." She handed me a piece of paper.

"Mental Health Hotline . . . how can I help?"

I told the nice lady about my fears, my hopelessness, the inconsideration of Doom and Gloom. She strongly suggested that I talk with someone, soon. But, I did that. Hello? Student Health? Scolding Lady? Hadn't-A-Clue Guy? Countless others? She gave me a name. Made me promise.

The therapist looked like someone I'd have invited over to my lunch table. She asked about my symptoms, my background, my family. When I told her my Cuban Missile Crisis story, she didn't laugh, or giggle.

"Why are you performing for me?" she said.

Ouch. Oh, she was good.

She asked me what my goals were, what I hoped to get out of our sessions? No one had ever asked me that.

"I want to be rid of Doom and Gloom. I want to feel alive. Not feel so . . . meh."

I talked with her for over an hour. Shed some tears. Popped a few emotional pustules. Maybe this time I'd be able to show Doom and Gloom the door? It was after our sixth session that she suggested anti-depressants.

Whoa. Whoa. Whoa.

I told her about my previous experience, how they made me *not* feel. She assured me that the new drugs – seratonin reuptake inhibitors – were different. She told me that my depression was really a chemical imbalance inside my brain. I had never thought of it that way. It made sense.

"It may take two, three weeks before you notice anything," she said.

I sat inside the car. Looking at her very legible hand writing.

"So . . . it's come to this?"

I knew that life inside my head was a mess. I mean, if I needed insulin, I'd take it. Or heart meds. I told my family to tell me if they noticed anything different about me. Good. Bad. Or nothing.

Day one? Doom and Gloom were still there, but had nothing to say.

Day two? They were in the other room with their door shut.

Day three? I remember waking up, feeling something was different. Good different. Lighter. Brighter. Doom? Gloom? Hello? They didn't answer. Had they gone? Where? I didn't know. I didn't care. For the first time since pre-Sister Gregory, I felt like the world was full of possibilities. I felt . . . like . . . me.

The reviews came trickling in.

More Fun To Be Around.

Better At Talking About Stuff.

No More Acting Like The Queen of Hearts.

Wait. What? Is that why my son hated Alice in Wonderland?

Four, five months . . . a year, three . . . several therapy sessions later, I felt bad. Not bad, bad, but bad that I hadn't done anything sooner. Oh, wait. That's right. I had. It took this long for me to find the right person, for science and the pharmaceutical companies to figure shit out.

I haven't seen or heard from Doom and Gloom in quite a while. Years. Almost a decade. Would it kill them to write? Drop me an email? I thought about making a friend request on Facebook . . . to see what they're up to . . . but . . . no. It's better this way.

Bificuration
by Diana M. Raab

Having a breast sliced off
leaves a woman with two lives—
the one before the loss
and the one after.

The post-op phantoms echo images
of a normal womanhood, stretching
back to the teen years and
horny pre-pubescent boys,
then passionate lovers
and husbands, all on the hunt
for mysterious erogenous zones.

My next life will be laden with
tears, eruptions of anger, reminders
of budding adolescence, the tinglings
of let-down and the sounds of a crying
baby who knows no other way to
ask for what it wants, unlike you
who have been in love for as many years
as your age now.

Shadow Texts
by Mike Smith

I still need you, my love.
The last line of an email I sent to Emily on December 1, 2009

Here is one odd thing I have done. For six and a half years, I have kept alive my late wife's Yahoo account. This was her personal email account, one that she tried not to access while at work, though if you were a particularly promising student of hers you might be given the address after graduation. As far back as grad school, I would mock her adamancy that work life and personal life be kept separate. In truth, she had an ability to compartmentalize, to prioritize, that I lacked and envied. About once a month, I log-in to this account and clean it up, sending to the trash the automatic updates from Target, Babies-R-Us, and Patagonia. In the beginning, I thought I might come across a friend from her childhood or adolescence who had not heard the news of her illness and death, but the news must have reached everyone because the only new personal emails sent to her account after her death were from me. Even after I married my second wife, Jennifer, I would send Emily messages, marking Langston's and Virginia's milestones or acknowledging dates that had been important to us: wedding anniversaries, the birthdays of family members, or what Virginia and Langston and I had done to commemorate Emily's own birthday. I sent her messages on the anniversary of our first date, which occurred before we admitted to ourselves that we were dating.

As time passed, it seemed acting as steward to this account might be another way I might preserve for our children something of Emily's voice in the emails she sent to her classmates from high school, college, and graduate school. But reading through these saved messages has made me realize, also, just how much of her voice I miss. As her health worsened over those four and a half months between diagnosis and death Emily moved increasingly towards silence. At the time, I thought this might be a consequence of having to adapt to our new roles as patient and caregiver, which was a reversal of our ten years together when every change of season seemed to wreck me for a week. Just what she thought about her illness, its roller-coaster progression, and all that seemed to leer at us no matter what treatment we might try, what fresh attitude we adopted, she kept to herself. Perhaps our new roles and the busyness of those months forced us into a new kind of intimacy, an intimacy that seemed to move beyond the need for speech. And it didn't trouble me then, this strange inwardness of Emily's, but I confess it has in the years after her death. It troubles me still.

Our relationship had little room for shared silence. Sometimes, it seemed, we fell in love across a counter top, hanging on each other's words, discussing everything. Part of the reason I loved her so deeply was because I felt she knew me better than I knew myself. She understood where I was coming from. Even when I didn't know what I was trying to say Emily could figure it out. Even before we started dating, our shifts at the bookstore were filled with talk. The bookstore was losing business steadily, so we had significant amounts of empty time to fill. It seemed we would never run out of things to share with one another. She had moved back home to apply to grad school. I was finishing up my last year of college. Both of our lives were in transition and we could almost see our futures opening up before us.

Conversation continued to ground us throughout our marriage. In graduate school, evening and late night talks replaced our Sunday mornings and we tried to meld our studies whenever we could. Emily decided to study Hebrew and German, and so we began translating psalms from the Dead Sea Scrolls and then set to work on Goethe's *Faust*. After Virginia was born, we struggled to give up the late night kitchen table chats and would exhaust ourselves swearing we wouldn't say another word as we lay beside each other in absolute darkness. So I was perplexed by Emily's silence, and tried hard to remember how terribly unfair it would be to let myself feel hurt.

Certainly, I kept things from her those months. I did not tell her that even before her diagnosis, the thoughts of all that might be going wrong with Emily and the pregnancy emerged in my quiet hours. I did not share with her the stories from the message boards dedicated to Stage IV Breast Cancer patients that I discovered as Emily began treatment and could not stop myself from visiting. I did not always answer her when she asked what had happened to the patient in a neighboring room and, for her part, she stopped asking. I did not tell her how hard I tried to purge from my memory the scene I witnessed during Emily's longest hospital stay. In the room cattycorner from us, a middle-aged Indian woman in traditional dress (petticoat and sari) sat for hours in a hospital chair staring straight ahead. A boy and girl, both under ten, sat unmoving and solemn-eyed on her lap. No one spoke. When I went to get my evening coffee, I saw the object of the family's attention. The man I presumed to be father and husband lay above the rumpled sheets and white blanket on the bed, in obvious agony. A plastic, disposable oxygen mask covered his nose and mouth, but the room had been emptied of all other equipment. He was conscious, his eyes fixed on the open door, though no nurse had entered or exited the room for quite some time. He was hours, perhaps minutes, from death. The art of medicine had been reduced to trying to ensure his comfort and wait patiently, passively, to clean and prep the room.

Against my will, I remained transfixed by this scene. Part of me resisted it as premonition; part of me took it as divine intervention:

tread carefully or this will come to pass for her as well. That it did come to pass, that the scene around my wife's deathbed also seemed ritualistic and symbolic to those who witnessed it, still makes me wonder what omen I failed to heed. And what god am I honoring by preserving my late wife's emails? It feels like a spiritual act, this stewardship, but to whom am I bringing pleasure? Clio, one of the nine muses, whose emblem is the scroll? Or Thoth, the self-begotten, who served as scribe to the Egyptian gods and was believed to be the author of every work ever written in every field of knowledge, human and divine? Or perhaps the scene I saw was sent by Sarasvita, who instills in pious Hindus a respect for all written works, so much so that should your toe stub itself on a cast down book, you owe it an apology? Or am I worshipping some new goddess, our goddess of hypertext, whose presence is felt by the lightning flash firing of the occipital nerve in heads bent too long over illuminated screens?

In any case, about once a month I find myself rereading the messages Emily sent during our time in D. C. In October of 2006, Emily emailed a new acquaintance to say she had volunteered to go to the pumpkin patch with Virginia's 4K class, and wouldn't be able to get "more than a utilitarian coffee" with her that day. A few days later she had to reschedule because I was out of town for a reading, and she had to wait for the heating maintenance guy to check the unit in our apartment. That same month, two students who had been particularly attached to her at Converse College, the school she'd taught at before Georgetown, wrote long emails, catching her up on all the events in their lives since last May. One was looking at law schools in the northeast and the other had moved to New York to work for a publishing house. Both made it clear that their lives would not have taken them in these directions had they not encountered Emily. Their exuberance, their desire to impress her and to let her know just how much she has meant to them seems to embolden the fonts as I read. "It's completely fascinating, and exactly something I can picture learning about in one of your classes". "You were so right to encourage me to bigger and better things than Spartanburg. I'm so unbelievably happy here, both in New York and at this place in my life. I feel like the entire world is at my fingertips, MUCH closer than it would have been from a desk in admissions at Converse."

Emily's response was her all over. "I love to hear about it all," she writes after lamenting that her response at the moment cannot be more "newsy" because she is completely swamped. She wants them to know, though, that she is "...well, proud is not the word as it is your effort and not mine, but I am happy about your choices and your future." Then, she obviously finds the time to make it newsier than she expected. "I think of you often, too...am planning a class and writing project about women, religion, and memoir in a year or two, and I will always associate you with that work because of all our time at Converse." What must have gone through Emily's mind was just how similarly she and I had been feeling since moving to D.C. three months before. Substitute D.C. for New York, and the email from her student might be one that Emily herself composed to *her* mentor. After all, only nine months had passed since we had made the trip back to South Bend in December so that Emily might defend her dissertation.

Many of the emails from that first semester, though, revolve around Virginia and me, our little family discoveries, the explorations of our new city, the nights out at Kavanagh's pizza and Max's Ice Cream, where Virginia bravely tried pumpkin ice cream for the first time and fell in love with it. There's a huge gap in the record of sent emails from December to April. These would have been difficult months, both physically and mentally, for Emily. I imagine most of her correspondence was conducted on her work email. After she'd been put on bed rest in March, she preferred the phone. On April 8, 2007, Easter Sunday, Emily broke her silence to write a long message to her friend, Janice, a fellow theologian from graduate school. Janice's husband and Emily had constituted their year's class in ethics, and the four of us had all gotten pretty close during their two shared years of coursework. Later, when Emily was pregnant with Virginia, Janice became her go-to person for help with negotiating the demands of pregnancy and childbirth with the strain of teaching for the first time. In fact, it was Janice who recommended we take classes on the Bradley method of natural childbirth, which had helped make Virginia's birth so magically hard.

Busy is the nature of these days of our lives, isn't it? I hope yours has been a happy busy—that the boys, and you and Bill are all healthy and doing well. Catch me up when you have some "spare" time. We are doing pretty good here... very busy. Our biggest news is that I am pregnant again... our BOY is due the first of August. So far, so good. Some pains and other small problems so I am staying off my feet as much as possible (as you must know this is easier said than done), and some very small worries from the ultrasound but we are trying to trust all will be resolved and turn out wonderfully. He is very active and responsive to everything already.

It's hard to read and reread this one particularly, in light of what happened, and I cannot help but compose shadow texts as palimpsest beneath Emily's words. Already Emily had been on bed rest for almost a month and her phrase "the pains and other small problems" was too brave a way of referencing the agony and deep worry of the last five months. Two and a half months later, as Emily and I were being transported by ambulance from Sibley hospital, where she had been slated to give birth, to Georgetown because it was more equipped to handle an emergency inducement, I remember wondering how they could expect her to go through a natural delivery when she was so clearly exhausted. We'd written an intricate birth plan five years before, even specifying that Bach's Cello Suites be played during the first stage. But we had not foreseen the forty-plus hours of labor Emily had endured before Virginia arrived. Although most of the thirty-six hours which elapsed between the time we learned of the urgency of the situation and Langston's actual birth weren't spent in active labor, Emily still suffered the low-grade discomforts of assessment and monitoring. I remember thinking, as we arranged care for Virginia and rushed to Sibley, that I would have to make it up to Emily after Langston arrived. She'd suffered so much for our family and my temper had been getting shorter and shorter with her. Even today, my stomach sinks when I remember joking to a friend (Can I really have said this?) that I wanted my next partner to be a more practiced stoic.

On April 10th, Emily wrote to my sister-in-law, about her newfound commitment to live in the present. I remember discussing this with her one night around this time. Virginia had finally fallen to sleep. Emily and I were sitting at our dining room table, luxuriating in the cool spring air and watching our dog, Jane, respond to the evening noises. I mentioned seeing the mother raccoon who had made her home in one of the tall oaks of the courtyard scamper to the gutter that evening, then quoted a line from a poem Emily had helped me with, "…Animal drift of the eternal present." This self-quoting was a mildly annoying habit of mine that I've since purged from my personality, and Emily stopped it gently with one of her sly smiles. This is the last night I remember in which we were something like our old selves together.

I am a little starved, stuck in my apt with only Michael and Virginia (and then Anne) to talk to. I think I am a little crazy (and a little angry and not very honest with myself about that). Anyway, maybe we will be able to talk about other things next time…I can't wait until next summer when we will be able to visit you guys up there. I can't believe I haven't seen your pretty place yet!

My new strategy (I'll let you know how it works out) is to try to see things more long-term. Not looking to the future for happiness (I am trying to live in the moment MORE) but to realize there will be plenty of time for lots of good things…that this period (mommy days) will last awhile and there will be other summers…

The subsequent message to my sister-in-law on April 19th breaks me in two.

I found myself with a few minutes before it is time for a pregnancy checkup this morning, so thought I'd email you. Present to the moment…a wonderful goal, but pretty hard I think. I am not good at it at all. My new attempt to see the big picture or whatever, is working ok, especially with work. But I have not been "present" to my own moments and certainly not to Michael…but we are working on it. An old friend just sent me a huge box of maternity clothes that included things like 10 of the same maternity t-shirts from Target (half in black). I feel rich. Well, off to take my achy bod to pee in a cup. This email turned out to be a bit blah, but there is a fog in my brain!

This email begins a whole series of exchanges, mostly utilitarian, full of baby lists and requests. Then, on June 14th, exactly one week from our anniversary and exactly two weeks before Langston will be induced, Emily writes to another old friend, one who will become indispensable to me over the next few years as I wrestle with the bureaucracy that accompanies widowers and single-parents:

Things are ok here…I developed gall bladder trouble in the last week or so and lost a lot of time and energy to feeling really rotten and going to the Doc. I think it is slowly getting better (though I have had to cut out all fat from my diet, which is much harder than I expected…not craving, but just thinking of things I can eat beyond fruit and veggies). But baby seems to be fine…at least that worry is getting better all the time.

Today is Virginia's last day of school, so I guess this afternoon she is a kindergartener! Crazy. Anne and Frank are coming early next week for a visit. I really hope it goes well...hope I feel like enjoying the company and hope Anne and I get along well...I've become very sensitive (easily irritated?) by things so I have to hope hard.

Michael and I are getting ready to celebrate our tenth anniversary next week too. He's taking me to a production of the Tempest and (if I can eat by then) out to dinner. He's hired a babysitter and everything—our first big grown-up D.C. outing.

The next email shocks me when I read it because I haven't noticed the date it was sent—August 4, twelve days after her diagnosis. She's writing to the same friend to confirm her plans to visit and help:

This will be quick as I am dopey and achy but all generally ok today. All your thoughts and notes mean so much.

The dates you suggested look great at this point—especially the 26th of August through the first of September or so—things of course change...I hope to go to Johns Hopkins for a second consultation, as yet unscheduled. Aug 27 V's first day and the 30th is another chemo session.

I hope a little of this makes sense b/c I can't sit here anymore.

The voice of the last email sent from the account takes me out of the place I go every time I dip back into these messages. The voice, its mechanical hope, repels me because it is my own. I'm writing to another old friend of Emily's who is coming into town, which means Emily is no longer able to respond.

It's too late to call, so this will have to do. Emily was

admitted back into the hospital today for a possible infection and they're likely to keep her there for at least a couple of days. We'll know more tomorrow. I know it's hard not to have your stomach sink when you here about these things, but the doctors seem to take this in stride and keep telling us that we're just going to have to find a way to get through these niggling hiccups, always keeping the bigger picture in mind.

And there have been encouraging developments. The chemo is working. One of her enzymes is now within normal limits and they're pretty sure the effect on the cancer has been "dramatic." For my part, I can tell you her liver, which once extended below her navel, is now back up where it's supposed to be under her ribcage. The ER docs thought so too.

All this means that you might be on your own getting from the airport to our apartment…Someone will be there to let you in, but it probably won't be me…Call our number when you get there, and someone will either come down or toss you the keys from the window.

The record of sent messages ends with my voice because the voice of the woman I loved has already fallen silent.

The Man Who Lives in My Shower
by Dallas Woodburn

There is a man who lives in my shower. He was here when I moved into my apartment three months ago, so I didn't have much choice in the matter. When I asked what he was doing lounging in the tub, he said, "First come, first serve." Which didn't really answer my question, but the man who lives in my shower is an enigmatic sort of fellow.

He leaves when I need to take a shower. (He's not *that* kind of man.) I don't know where he goes – the living room, I suppose, or the kitchen. Perhaps he simply sits on the counter beside the bathroom sink, waiting for me to be done. But he hides from me outside the bathroom. I only see him when he's in my shower.

* * *

The Realtor Woman – "Call me Kym" – who sold me the apartment wore maroon lipstick, smudged slightly on her top lip and electric-yellow high heels that emphasized the drab paleness of her skin. As she led me from entryway to dining alcove to bedroom she seemed to stomp each foot with angry emphasis, but when relating some crucial point about window lighting or square footage her smile flared like the flashbulb of a camera. We both knew she was asking too much for the apartment. She spoke to me in the tone of the celebrity chef assuring the audience how simple it is to make triple-layer cheesecake with seedless raspberry sauce – trying to convince the audience that they too can add meaning to the chaos of their lives by baking a perfectly textured dessert. In this case, my dessert was the liberated possibility of my life if I chose to live in apartment 3B at 2697 29th Street.

The apartment was above a Mexican/Greek/Ethnic restaurant where I imagined trying exciting new foods and becoming friends with the owners (undoubtedly a friendly old immigrant couple who would throw in free sides of baklava or bean salad and call me "mija"); the kitchen window looked out onto a quiet street, a block or two away from a tree-shaded park, where I could take walks in the evenings or mornings or afternoons, if I became the type of person who takes walks. Maybe I would get a dog, and then I would have a reason to go on walks. A dog would probably do me good. I could use some company.

"I'll take it," I told the Realtor Woman. Her smile slipped for a moment into a round "o" of surprise at my abruptness. After all, we hadn't even reached the bathroom yet ("Just wait till you see the gor-ge-ous tile work the previous owners put in around the tub!"). But, like the celebrity chef turning back to the cameras after a commercial break, she regained her composure and rebooted her smile. *Say cheese!* I was momentarily blinded by the flash, and stars twinkled in my vision as I signed the lease agreement.

* * *

It's been two months, and I think the man who lives in my shower is becoming more comfortable with my presence – my slippers in the doorway, my bathrobe on the hook behind the door, my face lotion and toothpaste on the bathroom counter – because lately he's started talking to me. Actually, he remarks on nearly everything I do. All from the bathroom, of course. He stays in the shower and shouts out commentary. Like this morning, as I walked past the bathroom – *My bedroom,* he reminds me, *please show some respect and knock first* – on my way down the hall to the kitchen, he yelled something I couldn't hear.

I paused, turned. "What?"

"Where are you going?" he asked, peeking out from behind the plastic shower curtain.

"I'm going to make breakfast."

"What are you making?" he asked.

"Toast."

"What kind?"

"Peanut butter. You want some?"

"No, thank you. I don't like the way you make toast."

"What? I make toast fine. How can you ruin toast?" I slipped a slice into the toaster and retraced my steps to the bathroom, standing outside the doorway so he couldn't see me in my faded flannel pajamas.

"It's not your toast, exactly. It's your bread. Why do you freeze your bread?"

"How do you know I freeze my bread?"

"I just know," he said. "But I don't understand it. Nobody likes frozen bread."

"I freeze it so it doesn't get all moldy. I can never eat a whole loaf by myself without it growing moldy."

"Can't you just buy a smaller loaf? Or split a loaf with a friend?"

"That's ridiculous. Who would I split it with? And why do you even care that I freeze my bread? It works for me."

"I hate to think of you prying frozen bread slices apart with your fingers. And then sometimes the crust gets all under your fingernails. Nobody likes that."

DING! The toaster chimed. I padded back to the kitchen.

"And besides," he shouted after me, "toast doesn't taste as good when you make it with frozen bread."

"I can't even tell," I shouted back. "I think it tastes de-lish-ous."

"That's only because you've gotten used to frozen bread," he said. "You forget what real toast tastes like."

* * *

"Why do you freeze your bread?" Ryan asked me in the last conversation we ever had. Actually, it wasn't the last conversation. We had one more conversation, later that night, but I don't like to think about that one.

I was making a sandwich for dinner, phone wedged between my chin and shoulder, and I complained about getting pieces of crust stuck underneath my fingernails when trying to pry two frozen slices apart.

"It gets all moldy if I don't freeze it," I explained. "I can't eat a whole loaf by myself without it getting moldy."

"That is the saddest thing I've ever heard," he said.

"Well, I'm pretty sad without you."

"I miss you too, babe," he said. "But someday we'll have a place of our own. And we won't have to freeze the bread. I'll make you fresh-bread sandwiches."

"Promise?"

"Promise."

The next day, he hung himself from his shower rod with his necktie.

* * *

It was the tie with the goldfish on it, the one I picked out for him right before he left for Detroit. I bought it because Ryan and I had a pet goldfish named Sparky. Most couples buy dogs, I know, but Ryan had horrible allergies. I didn't really mind. I liked watching little Sparky in his glass bowl beside our tiny kitchen sink. I liked the way the sunlight from the window reflected off the water and the way he swam to the surface and darted at the flakes of food I carefully shook out for him each morning and night.

When I found out about Ryan's accident – that's the word my mind still clings to, *accident* – I thought, of course, that there must be some mistake. Ryan was happy. It was a farce, a fake, a framing.

Later, when the detail surfaced about the goldfish necktie, my stomach tightened and something inside me congealed into recognition. Ryan left no note. But I know the goldfish necktie was meant for me.

Exactly one week later, I woke up to Sparky floating belly-up in his little glass bowl, surrounded by uneaten food flakes. I couldn't bear to flush him down the toilet, so I buried him in the tiny backyard, underneath the hydrangea bushes.

Before the hydrangeas had lost their blooms, my life was packed into boxes. I said goodbye to that tiny house on Hayward Avenue and moved into a tinier apartment on Figueroa and Twenty-Ninth. I came home from work one evening to the unmistakable sound of shower water running.

"Yoo hoo, is someone home? Excuse me? Do you have any shampoo?" a voice called from the bathroom. "I'm all out."

And that is how I met the man who lives in my shower.

* * *

The man who lives in my shower is shaving his moustache. I'm glad; I'm not a fan of moustaches. It looked okay on him, because he always kept it neatly trimmed. But shaving is definitely an improvement. I tell him so.

"Thanks," he says. "I think."

His whiskers fall into the bathroom sink. Some drift sluggishly across the counter. "You're going to clean this up, right?" I ask.

"Of course. What kind of roommate do you think I am?" He turns to face me, half his moustache gone and the other half covered in white foam. I am about to laugh, but then I see it.

The goldfish necktie. He's wearing the goldfish necktie.

"Wait ... you're ... the necktie." I point.

He looks at it, holds it up between his thumb and index finger, lets it flap back down. He shrugs.

My tongue is itchy. "The necktie. Where'd you ... where'd you get that?"

He smiles. "You gave it to me."

"That's ridiculous!" I'm shrieking now. "I never gave that to you! Where'd you find it? Huh? Where?"

He shakes his head. "I won't be here much longer, Bee. Please, let's not waste time arguing." He turns back to his half-shaved moustache. His eyes, in the mirror, flit towards mine; he holds my gaze for a moment, as if to see whether I understand.

I don't.

He looks away.

I stumble to my room, shut the door, and crumble into a heap on the bed, thinking of the way he would lazily run his finger around the lip of Sparky's fish bowl when we were talking in the tiny kitchen after dinner. I'd be washing the dinner dishes and watching him out of the corner of my eye, his finger lightly making circles around and around and around that fishbowl, and it was all I could do to keep my knees from shaking. Usually I managed to set the last dish on the counter to dry, rinse the soapsuds off my hands, and smooth my hair flat before I calmly took his hand and led him into the bedroom. Once, though – the day he finally shaved his god-awful moustache – I hadn't washed but one wine glass and a frying pan before I couldn't take it any longer. I grabbed him in front of Sparky, right there in that tiny kitchen.

Tell me, isn't that what happiness is? A shiny goldfish in its bowl, hydrangea bushes in bloom, someone to love who can't even wait to finish washing the dinner dishes to love you right back?

* * *

When people used to ask about my engagement, I liked to tell them that it was both the happiest and saddest day of my life. Happiest because it was the day Ryan asked me to be his wife. Saddest because in the next breath he told me he was leaving.

"Jerry chose me to go to Detroit, Bee," he said.

I blinked. "What?"

"He needs to send someone, and he thinks I'm the best candidate. He told me after work today." Ryan looked up at me, still awkwardly perched on one knee beside the bed. His hands, lying palm-up on the bedspread, seemed lonely without the shiny satin ring box cradled in them.

"I don't ... I don't understand. When?"

"Three weeks."

"Wow. That's soon."

"I know – I know it is. But listen, Bee – it's only for a year. Just until you finish school. Then you can come out and join me."

"In Detroit?"

"Yeah – or, you know, wherever they transfer me after that. You know how versatile sales is. Branches close and other branches open. They send you somewhere new. But that doesn't matter. Really, Bee. Because we'll be together. Right? Look at me, Bee."

I looked down into Ryan's earnest hazel eyes, at the tiny mole above his left eyebrow and the crooked part in his floppy dark hair, and the tears that had been welling up in my eyes leaked free, blurring my contact lenses. Happy tears and sad tears all muddled together. He reached up and brushed my cheek with his thumb. Cupped my chin in his palm.

"You and me, Bee. That's all. That's all that matters."

"A year's not so long," I said. "I guess a year isn't so long."

He hugged me then, and kissed me, and it wasn't until he died that I realized I'd never actually said yes.

* * *

I have a new saddest day now, of course. And though the ring still clings to my left ring finger, I don't think of it as my engagement ring anymore. *Till death do us part.* What a silly promise, that death could part two people. Death means love grips tighter, suffocates, becomes laced with regret. And regret is messy. It clings to you.

Till death do us part. What a morbid, terrifying thing to say at a wedding. Of course, we didn't make it to our wedding, so Ryan and I never promised that death would part us. Maybe that's why it hasn't. Maybe that's why he refuses to leave.

Now, if ever anyone asks about my engagement ring, I pretend

not to hear. Nobody likes a suicide, especially when they're
expecting a wedding.

* * *

A golden strip of light creeps out beneath the bathroom door.
I knock softly, twice, then step inside. The man who lives in my
shower is perched on the side of the tub, a stack of crumpled white
pages in his lap. He looks up and nods hello.

"I didn't know you could read," I say.

"What made you think I couldn't?"

"Nothing. I don't know."

"You didn't think ghosts could read?" he asks. "Is that it?"

"Are you a ghost?"

The man in my shower gives me a half-smile, but doesn't say
anything. He shuffles the papers and continues to read.

I watch him. Did his hair always flop over his eyes in that way,
the part slightly crooked? I search for the tiny mole, the one over
his left eyebrow, but it's difficult to see in this light.

"What are you reading?"

He glances up. "Your short story."

Blood throbs in my temples. "What story?"

He flips back to the first page. "It doesn't have a title."

Not that one. I reach in and with one swift motion grab the
papers from him. "How did you get this?"

He blinks up at me like a startled child. "You gave it to me, Bee.
Remember?"

"I don't know what you're talking about. I never – "

"Who is this guy, Bee?"

"What guy?"

"Who is this guy in your story?"

I stare at him for a moment. His eyes look more green than
hazel, but maybe it's just the light. I shove the papers at him and
slam the door behind me.

* * *

"Who is this guy, Bee?"

His voice on the other end of the line was small and tight. I pictured his words with little curlicues of anger, scribbling their way into my ears.

"What guy? What are you talking about, Ry?"

"You know exactly what I'm talking about. This guy. In your story."

"My story – Ryan, that's fiction –"

"Who is he? Don't lie to me. I've read your other stuff. You always base your stories in real life. You even told me that, remember? God!" I heard the muffled sound of something falling. I pictured Ryan kicking a chair, knocking it over.

"Ryan. Listen to me. There is no one else."

"Shut up. You could at least be honest with me." He was breathing hard and his words were slurred.

"Have you been drinking? You're being ridiculous. I am being honest, Ry!"

"Then who is this guy?"

"I based him on you, okay? You."

"Liar!" Another loud crash.

"Ryan, calm down. I'm not lying to you."

"I have hazel eyes."

"I know you do."

"I have hazel eyes and this guy in the story has blue eyes."

"So? I just changed your eye color –"

"*Your eyes are so big, like the eyes of a little boy, blue as a perfect robin's egg –*"

"Ryan –"

"*Looking into your eyes, it's as if I can curl up and fall asleep inside them –*"

"Stop it –"

"*Safe, warm. Protected –*"

"Ryan, I sent you my story because I want you to be a part of my life out here. I want to share my work with you. I want your support. I'm having that story workshopped next Thursday and I was hoping you could give me suggestions –"

"Here's a suggestion: why don't you go show it to your other boyfriend?"

"I'm not going to argue about this with you anymore."

"Just because I'm far away doesn't mean you can parade around like a fucking slut –"

I hung up. I thought about calling him back right away, but decided instead to watch an episode of *Friends*. Give him a chance to calm down, I thought. Sober up. Then I would call him back. It was the *Friends* episode with the fake Monica. After the ending theme music swelled, I dialed Ryan's home number, then his cell. But by then there was no answer.

Of all my regrets, that stupid episode of *Friends* is the hardest to keep buried.

The last two words he ever said to me were *fucking slut*. That is why I don't like to think about our final conversation. That is why I still eat frozen bread. And that is why I dropped out of my MFA program and stopped writing altogether.

* * *

I found out later that Ryan had gotten demoted at his job that day. His boss said he had been coming in late, leaving early, missing sales calls. A couple of his coworkers thought he was depressed and suggested he see a shrink, but Ryan never wanted help from anyone. Especially not from me. He was good at hiding. He gave a remarkable performance, at least until the very end. That was the only time I got a small peek behind the curtain.

And what did I do? I hung up the phone.

* * *

Midnight. I can't sleep. I slip into the kitchen, heave open the refrigerator door. Hummus, yogurt, ketchup, milk. Leftover chicken and rice in a plastic container, a condensation of water droplets on the inside of the lid. I close the refrigerator door.

Padding back to my empty room, I notice the golden strip of light still creeping out beneath the bathroom door. I tip-toe up and press my ear against the thin wood door. Nothing. My heart seems to beat very loudly. I hesitate, my fist inches from the wood, and then I knock softly, twice. Nothing. I slowly open the door and step inside. For a half-instant, I'm terrified that I'll see his body, hanging lifelessly from the shower rod.

But the man who lives in my shower is perched harmlessly on the side of the tub. Has he moved at all in the seven hours since I stormed out on him this evening? He is wearing the goldfish necktie, but it is unthreateningly loose around his neck. He is still holding the stack of crumpled white pages in his lap. He looks up at me.

"Hi," I say. My voice is dry and croaky.

"Hi, Bee."

I look at my toes as I walk towards him. My nails are painted pink, the polish chipped around the edges. I sit beside him on the rim of the bathtub. It is filled with sudsy water, cold to the touch. Now my hand has soapsuds on it; I wipe it off on my striped pajama pants. I glance down at the page the man who lives in my shower is reading. It is the same page from earlier. *"I love you," you say. We're lying together on my bed and you turn on your side to look at me. Your eyes are so big, like the eyes of a little boy, blue as a perfect robin's egg. Looking into your eyes, it's as if I can curl up and fall asleep inside them. Safe, warm. Protected.*

"I love you, too," I say. I've said it before, to other people, but nobody's eyes are as blue as yours, and I realize with a flood of piercing certainty that until this moment I've never really meant it. I look at him, finally. His eyes are hazel. His part is crooked. He looks exactly the same as the last day I saw him, hugging goodbye at the airport. He held me so tightly, I remember thinking for a moment that I couldn't breathe. As if he was trying so desperately

to hold onto something. I should have known, then. How could I not have known?

"How could I not have known?" I ask. Warm tears gather around my eyes.

"I didn't want you to know."

"But why not? I could have helped. I could have ... Things could have been different."

He sighs. "I wanted to be perfect for you. I couldn't bear for you to see me in such a bad place."

He drops a page of my story into the bathtub. The page fills up with water and sinks. The ink blurs. He drops a second page, then a couple more.

"I was so mad at you," I say. "I was furious at you. How could you do that? How could you leave me like that?"

"It was a mistake." Another page drifts lazily down into the sudsy water. "You have to believe me. I didn't mean to leave you. I'm sorry, Bee. I'm so sorry."

My nose is running, my eyes burning with angry tears. I wipe them away with the back of my hand. "And that's supposed to make it all okay?" My voice is louder than I intended.

"You can't go on living like this forever."

I don't say anything.

"Frozen bread and ghosts won't do."

His hazel eyes gleam the same way they did when he told me he was leaving for Detroit. I know his next words before he says them: "It's time for me to go." Only, I realize now, there was something else there before, a flicker of fear that I mistook for anxious exhilaration. That isn't there now. His face is calm. His eyes are unclouded.

"Goodbye." He leans down and kisses my forehead, softly. Just a slight pressure, like the gentle push of an index finger against the small of your back, but it's more than I can bear. I waver and tumble backwards into the bathtub, bumping my elbow against one of the faucet knobs and sitting down hard on my tailbone. The soggy pages of my short story, unfinished and untitled – the last words I wrote – drift around me. I shiver. I pry off my sopping shirt, strip away my cotton pajama pants. I gather the pages of my short story into a comforting weight against my chest. Only then do I glance up at the man who used to live in my shower. He smiles at me from the bathroom doorway.

"Goodbye, Ryan," I say. "I'm sorry, too."

"You have nothing to be sorry for."

"I love you."

"I love you, Bee. I always will." And then he is gone.

* * *

I have a dog now from the Humane Society. A golden retriever. His name is Fitz, after F. Scott Fitzgerald. *The Great Gatsby* is my favorite book, though Ryan could never get through it. I think he would have liked my Fitzgerald, though. He would have liked to see me take Fitz on walks through the park. We stop at a bench overlooking the playground. Fitz curls on the ground near my feet. I sit sideways, with my knees up on the seat, and tilt my face to the winter sunshine. I gently open the cover of my worn spiral notebook, smooth flat a fresh page, and place the tip of my pen against the emptiness. It will take a long time to fill it, I know. But I begin.

Carrion Comfort
by Gerard Manley Hopkins

Not, I'll not, carrion comfort, Despair, not feast on thee;
Not untwist - slack they may be - these last strands of man
In me ór, most weary, cry I can no more. I can;
Can something, hope, wish day come, not choose not to be.
But ah, but O thou terrible, why wouldst thou rude on me
Thy wring-world right foot rock? lay a lionlimb against me? scan
With darksome devouring eyes my bruisèd bones? and fan,
O in turns of tempest, me heaped there; me frantic to avoid thee and flee?

Why? That my chaff might fly; my grain lie, sheer and clear.
Nay in all that toil, that coil, since (seems) I kissed the rod,
Hand rather, my heart lo! lapped strength, stole joy, would laugh, chéer.
Cheer whom though? the hero whose heaven-handling flung me, fóot tród
Me? or me that fought him? O which one? is it each one? That night, that year
Of now done darkness I wretch lay wrestling with (my God!) my God.

Evening

"The most beautiful people we have known are those who have known defeat, known suffering, known struggle, known loss, and have found their way out of the depths. These persons have an appreciation, a sensitivity, and an understanding of life that fills them with compassion, gentleness, and a deep loving concern. Beautiful people do not just happen."

—Elisabeth Kübler-Ross, *Death: The Final Stage of Growth*

Intersection
by Jason Brown

The sun had faded the stop sign pink,
and on windy days, the thin metal quivered
on a wooden pole,
                an unsteady wave goodbye

at the line of vehicles in my father's rearview mirror
entering the north side of town after work, one
                       stop-and-go at a time,

and for fifteen years my father turned right,
away from our house, to visit my grandfather,

who didn't even peek over his newspaper
              folded apart with open arms
when we walked through the living room
without knocking.

My father's coffee cup sat across the table,
already full, steam curling above its lip.
They divided the paper and drank
                          without talk,
a long silence about working the railroad yards
(one retired, one about to) each with pliers
in brown leather cases hooked on their belts,
welding scars like smashed strawberries
on their forearms.

I never joined them at the table.

A week later, I couldn't stop
staring into my grandfather's casket,

his hands cold and calloused on his chest,
a right-over-left handshake with himself,
his index fingers stained yellow
from unfiltered tobacco
                    smoked on the back patio.

I gently squeezed his earlobe
and his face turned into my father,

who stood before me and the pink lily wreaths.
I wrapped my arms around him from behind
and squeezed.
        He patted my shoulder
like patting himself on the back.

We grandsons slid the casket in and out
of the black-slick hearse, into the grave,
as if we were just moving furniture around,

and I thought about my father, the pink stop sign
and how the next day he had to drive home from
work,
                    the turn he would take.

Sonya Sweeping
by Jennifer Highland

This is how you find her:
hands clamped around the broom handle
like a bulldog's teeth,
working the farthest corners of the room
till the dust spins around her like a fast-forward galaxy
all sparkly where the light comes through.

You watch those dead and broken bits of her
drift and churn with each stroke.

Sonya sweeping.
Sonya weeping
little dribs out the edges of her eyes—
you know that mood

where everything's so fallen-down
all you want is to make something clean.

When you try to call her name Sonya
hears only her own two feet
crunching an iced-over lane.
Her spine looks dry like a leaf in the wind.

You want to reach her,
far-away Sonya,
tell her she's worth saving

stretch your arms way down
into the gray-green murk closing
over her head, saying hang on girl

'cause Sweetness, even your dust
knows how to shine.

Checking in With a Griever
by Alexandra Rosas

-Day 1 Friday:

11:00 a.m. Mother's funeral. Wear black dress. Deliver eulogy with voice breaking only at last sentence. Host luncheon.

11:52 a.m. Survive.

2:15 p.m. Pack minivan up with photo boards, candles and crystal dishes from mother's service. Take impulsive exit off freeway to drop off 300 Stargazer Lilies from funeral. Try to tell mother's headstone how beautiful they are but sob incoherently instead.

3:40 p.m. Arrive back home. Fall into back door then fall face down onto sofa. Hold youngest son, who lets me.

5:50 p.m. Wake up from nap in black dress from mother's funeral. Family never asks if I'm going to change out of nice dress.

7:13 p.m. Stare into space from sofa. Hear family tiptoe around me.

10:05 p.m. Ask son to bring down pillow. Sleep on sofa in black dress from mother's funeral. Pray for dream with mother.

-Day 2 Saturday:

8:01 a.m. Wake up in black dress from funeral.

7:00 p.m. Change from black dress into black T-shirt.

7:15 p.m. Drive self in black T-shirt and slippers for something to eat. Only want ice cream.

8:20 p.m. Friend drops off purple violet plant, my mother's favorite. Can barely make out velvety leaves through blur of tears.

9:05 pm. Go into garage, stare at van full of things from mother's funeral, no room for driving with children. Walk back into house, exhausted.

9:10 p.m. Turn to Facebook: van needs emptying. Unable to do. Sage friends advise children to empty items into back room.

9:39 p.m. Children do as asked. Put off going through items until later.

11:41 p.m. Fall asleep grateful for wise friends on Facebook.

-Day 3 Sunday:

7:48 a.m. Open eyes to view from sofa of startling blue sky through raindrops!

7:49 a.m. Shout at kids to be dressed and ready to go because *Now! Now!* is perfect weather for visit to cemetery. Everyone obeys.

9:45 a.m. Visit cemetery and cry softly with children's arms around me. Drive home, radio on but can't understand words. Hear my own words in my head of how one week ago she was with me.

Want today to be someone else's life.

12:30 pm. Son suggests movies. Escape from my life with him. He lets me rest my head on his shoulder during previews, and then throughout movie. He doesn't re-adjust for comfort or go to the bathroom once despite large soda.

6:30 p.m. Dear friend drops off pizza and salad. Take three bites and swallow hard in between lump in throat.

11:07 p.m. Promise to re-send, re-write, re-word every sympathy card ever sent to anyone who has lost a mother. Will begin with, "My apologies, I had no idea."

-Day 4 Monday:

6:49 a.m. On sofa, eyes open, body tired but mind too sad to sleep. Still in black T-shirt from weekend.

7:20 a.m. Dear friend knocks on door and drops off card. Is taken aback by sight of me, words spill before she can stop them. Endears herself to me by stammering, "I like the T-shirt you've been wearing these days."

12:00 p.m. Take children with me to funeral home to pick up mother's cremains. Even with evidence of her ashes in my hands, my mind says not her.

12:40 p.m. Children save my life by making me laugh on drive home when littlest says, "Who me? Oh, you know, nothing special -- just driving around with my grandmother's ashes in the minivan."

1:30 p.m. Ice cream for lunch.

6:47 p.m. And dinner.

-Day 5 Tuesday:

7:15 p.m. Place mother's ashes in car seat next to me and go for ice cream. Cry while driving, wondering who's going to ask me now about the stories in my life.

7:35 p.m. Park car at mother's favorite ice cream drive-in and begin with what was always her first question to me as soon as I walked into her room at hospice, for the latest story of woman who is thorn in my side. Salty tears fall and mix into my chocolate ice cream as I talk to her. I tell her what's new. I finish cone.

8:00 p.m. 18-year-old son gets surprising new job of hearse driver when mother's ashes are left in car from ice cream run earlier in evening. He takes car, and thus inadvertently takes her for ride with him. He comes home saying, "Well, looks like Nona finally got to go for that car ride alone with me."

8:09 p.m. Bring my mother's ashes in, place her in piano room, where she can now sit near front window, listening to her grandchildren's serenades.

9:00 p.m. Change into grey T-shirt.

11:50 p.m. Sofa feels least loneliest sleeping spot in house. Able to see mother's ashes from across the room. On side, in grey T-shirt, with knees up to chest. Wonder what I'm going to do with cracked heart.

4:15 a.m. Wake with crick in my neck and see littlest next to me. Don't want him to wake and leave so let him stay in my neck cranny.

-Day 6 Wednesday:

7:15 a.m. Take Tylenol for crick in neck from littlest sleeping in there all night. Rest of morning: remain in T-shirt.

9:21 a.m. On sofa, chanting to self a grade school cheer *Get up! Get going! You can move and do it! Goooooooooo me!*

10:19 a.m. Force self to shower. Time disappears in warm water. Need to register two oldest for high school. Come back home needing rest. Leave in afternoon for school shoes for children.

1:55 p.m. Return home and pat self on back for shoe shopping completed, and only answering three people who asked about summer with, "My mother died." Flop down on sofa.

2:05 p.m. Call littlest over and scoop him in my arms. Bury my face in his soft head. We fall asleep.

-Day 7 Thursday:

10:40 a.m. Try singing along to radio but voice won't go faster than 33 rpm.

3:00 p.m. Attempt to do laundry and grocery shopping but legs are stiff and arms leaden. Will try again Friday.

5:25 p.m. Five pounds chocolate covered raspberries for dinner.

1:00 a.m. Order T-shirt from Zazzle, "I have no parents. Be nice."

1:20 a.m. Set alarm to wake at 6:45 a.m. then plan to go to small bakery downtown and buy all the donuts they have.

1:50 a.m. Take blanket to sofa, stare at ceiling and marvel that seven days have passed. Life is strange, untethered, without a mother. Hot tears slip from the sides of my eyes and puddle in my ears because I don't know what I'm going to do now that the person who loved me more than anything, is gone.

* * *

Day 17 Update: *Continuing to survive the ups and downs. Dealing with troubled moments that strike out of nowhere when you are at your weakest. Not able to walk past the watermelon at the supermarket because breakfasts with my mother always began with me bringing over a bowl of chilled, cubed watermelon. Coconut water aisle especially painful, because she had just discovered she had a love of coconut water, and had only been able to love it for three weeks.*

Why Are You Depressed, He Asks
by Katie Manning

There's never just one answer. Everything pushes
down at once, like my body leaves a canyon
in the bed, deeper each night. I will never know
Chinese, just the charred bones of dismembered
language, unremembered. My face will never cause
whole nations to fall in love or in war. My words
turn no men to swine. Sometimes I'm content.
Sometimes I wish some god would turn my flesh
to tree bark thighs firm, bird song in my hair.

Lymph Nodes, Liver Lesions and My Mother
by Sarah Cooper

As the doctor exits the exam room she reaches for my hand. I pull her entire body onto my lap as she continues to stare at the Gastrointestinal Diagram like a map of the stars, searching for constellations, seeing only organs, glands and tissues. "Do I need my liver to live?" I stare at her, feeling her sit bones press into my quivering quads. Her hands interlocked around my shoulders like a child asking if she has to get the flu shot. "Let's try to keep it," I offer. I hold her against me, smelling the skin between her clavicle and neck, and watching a vein pulse. "Everything is going to be okay", I persist but what I wanted to say is: *No matter what, it's an honor to take this ride with you.*

A Talent for Ironing
by Carol Wobig

After brushing aside a cobweb, Marge headed down the basement stairs, careful to set her foot in the center of the warped boards. In the blurry light from the glass block windows, she wrestled the medium-sized ladder out of the dark space beneath the stairs.

Now, to get herself and the ladder up the stairs. She did it one step at a time, stopping to get her breath and cursing Fred all the way. He should be here to help her. By the time she got to the top, sweaty and thankfully in her oldest housedress, she had to sit down at the table and have a cup of coffee, and a donut.

She held her breath when a car clattered down the street. Exhaled. The car didn't stop. She'd told Debbie she wouldn't be home today, because she would be cleaning at church. For a younger sister, Debbie was very bossy, always had been. A lot of days when she was with her, Marge had to bite the inside of her cheek to stop mean thoughts from flying out of her mouth.

Like yesterday.

They were at McDonald's having a senior coffee. Marge's was legal. Debbie had lied to get the reduced price.

"I don't think you should live alone anymore," Debbie said.

This conversation again.

"And why is that?" Marge asked. "Do you think I'm losing it?" She was not losing it, and she had no intention of hanging around until she did.

"No. You're not losing it. I just worry about you alone in that big old house with all the stairs."

"Oh you worry too much," Marge said, "Take a bite."

"No, thanks."

"Good. There's more for me."

"You should lose some weight."

The other usual topic of conversation.

"I know," Marge said. She could feel her belly resting on the top of her thighs. Maybe if Fred had lost weight, he'd still be here. With the last bite of the roll, she scraped up the dribbles of frosting left in the corners of the box.

Today, after the work of getting the ladder up the stairs, she ate another donut, the one intended for Fred. "My fat is all your fault," she said to the air, though the pounds had been there long before he died. Who knew she would miss him so much? But today she had work to do.

In the dining room, she stood the ladder up next to the window and after brushing off the thin line of dust that topped each drape, removed them from the rod. The material, navy blue with white cabbage roses, was faded in places, but there was enough toward the bottom to make her funeral dress.

She laid the panels out on the dining room table, removed the hooks, and ripped the stitches out of the pleats. She trimmed away the good material. There was enough to make a dress with a gored skirt, an out-of-date style, but most of it wouldn't show anyway. She made a pattern out of the Want Ads of the Sunday paper, pinned it to the material, and saw herself laid out in the dress, her pearls resting on the navy material, a rosary entwined in her waxy fingers. Yes. That would all do.

The next morning, her whole body ached. She'd stayed up until midnight sewing. The gored skirt took a lot of time; she'd almost changed her plan, but didn't want to spend good money on a burial dress. Before she got back to the sewing, she opened the front door, coffee in hand, to check the weather.

Snowflakes drifted down and melted on the still-green grass, all the more beautiful because soon she wouldn't have to worry about getting the sidewalk shoveled. All she really had to worry about was how to end it all. She didn't want to damage her face—she did want to look good in the casket. And she had to do it without anyone knowing it was her choice. The Catholic Church didn't look kindly on suicide. It sent you straight to hell, and you couldn't have a Mass and be buried in the church's cemetery. Maybe pills. She had a stash of Fred's in the nightstand. How many would she need to take? How could she find that out? She didn't know. She had to get back to work.

By lunchtime, the skirt was complete. After a peanut butter sandwich and a piece of blueberry pie, a la mode, she went to the front door to check the snowfall. It was piling up, and across the street on the strip of grass next to the curb, there was what? — a piano? Yes, a piano, a battered upright, a loose tarp hanging over the top. A fine layer of snow drifted onto the keys. How foolish. They could have sold it.

She went back to the dining room and worked on the dress, made a simple top, a collarless v-shaped bodice with raglan sleeves. Marge still used her mother's old Singer. The up and down motion of the treadle, the efficiency of the needle traveling along the edge of the material, a comfort. She'd been close to her mother in an odd way. Had wanted her approval, something she'd never managed to earn. But that didn't matter now. She was tired. She was done.

Marge was ready to attach the bodice to the skirt, but needed a break. Stretching, she checked on the piano. A yellow piece of construction paper, wilting in the snow, had been taped to the side. Black lettering said "FREE." Marge had always wanted to play the piano. But it was too late. Her fingers were stiff with arthritis most days, and she had other plans.

After supper, the dress was complete. Before she got into her nightgown, she gave it a try. When a pin she'd forgotten scraped the soft flesh of her under arm and brought tears to her eyes, she had to sit on the edge of the bed and pull herself together before she looked in the mirror. Fred would have approved. Sweet man that he was he'd learned to never say yes when she asked him if an outfit made her look fat.

The next morning, before she went down to the kitchen, she looked out the upstairs window. The tarp had been lowered to cover the keys. The sign lay crumpled in a snow bank.

The piano, the piano. Stop. She had more important things to think about.

As she fried herself an egg, Debbie yoo-hooed from the front door. She never knocked.

"I was going to shovel your sidewalk, but I see it's done."

"The neighbors. Sit down. I'll make you some breakfast."

"Thanks. Just an egg. No toast. What's with that piano across the street?"

"It's been there since yesterday. It's free. There was a sign on it."

"I think I'll give it a try when I leave. Jeremy might like it."

Marge nodded, didn't say that maybe her grandson would like it, too, a thought that hadn't occurred to her before this moment.

After breakfast, Debbie walked across the street, reached under the tarp and played a few chords, gave Marge a thumbs up on the way back to her car. Marge felt her blood pressure rise. Damn her sister. Always taking everything for herself.

When Debbie's car turned the corner, Marge put on her boots and coat, hustled across the street and rested the tips of her fingers on the keys. They were cold, like the ones she'd been allowed to touch only under her mother's supervision. Marge's chore was to dust the keys every week with a thin cloth, careful never to push them down. Her dad slept during the day, and came roaring out of the bedroom, belt in hand, if she or her brothers woke him.

"Could I take lessons, too?" Marge asked one night after her dad had gone to work. She was doing her math homework at the kitchen table while Debbie practiced and her mother made supper.

"Oh, honey, I wish you could. But there's only money for one of you, and Mrs. Wright says that Debbie has the talent."

Marge wasn't sure what that meant, talent. But it didn't seem to be making the noise coming out of the dining room any better than it had sounded yesterday.

But this morning, standing next to the piano in the snow, she was alone. No mother. No father. She pushed one key down. Another. Another. When the front door of the house behind the piano opened, she drew her hand back like she'd touched a hot burner.

A young woman in a sweatshirt, jeans, and slippers came down the shoveled walk and stood next to her. "You can have that," she said. "The people we bought the house from left it behind. Neither of us can play." She smiled and patted her belly. "We need the room for the baby." She extended her hand to Marge. "I'm Tina."

"Nice to meet you, I'm Marge." Marge touched Tina's warm hand. "Sorry – I know my hand's cold. Why did you put the piano out in the snow?"

"We weren't paying attention to the weather report." She laughed. "We wanted to get it out of the way so we could paint."

"Pink or blue?" Marge smiled at Tina and then brushed the snow off a few more keys.

"Yellow. We're waiting to see what we're having."

"That's good. How Fred and I did it." She rested her finger on Middle C, the only key she could identify.

"Would you like the piano? Maybe your kids could move it for you."

Tina pulled a piece of twine out of her pocket. Together, they laid the tarp back in place, tied it down.

"I'm not sure. I'd have to hire movers. My son is in California. Could I think about it for an hour or two?"

"Sure. Sure." She shivered. "I'm freezing. I have to go in. Talk to you later."

"Okay." Marge stepped onto the street.

"Marge," Tina called from her front door. "I'll get my husband and his friends to move it for you if you want it."

Marge turned and waved, extinguished a small light that had flickered in her chest for a moment, and focused on getting into her house without falling on the ice.

The dress lay on the ironing board in front of the dining room, ready to be pressed for the last time. She turned on the iron and sat down for a cup of coffee.

Fred would think she was crazy. Debbie would, too. She was crazy. Why had she said she would think about it? What would she do with a piano? Where would she put it? No, the piano would go to Debbie.

Steam rose from the iron, took her back to her childhood home. She pressed each gore, first on the inside, then on the outside. She did have a talent for ironing. Mother had told her that over and over. At first, Marge had pressed her father's handkerchiefs, eventually she was allowed to do his shirts. As she smoothed the right raglan sleeve of her dress, she looked up. The windows needed to be cleaned, but with the drapes removed to make the dress, she could see the sunset through the bushes Fred had planted years ago. This would be a good place for a piano. She could look up into the trees when she practiced. When she practiced? What was she thinking?

Practicing?

She walked to the front door. The piano was still there. She walked back to the dining room, imagined it standing against the windows, herself sitting there, practicing.

Yes, practicing.

She laid the perfectly ironed dress over her arm, carried it up the stairs, zipped it into a plastic garment bag, and hung it in the back of the closet.

It could wait.

Biographies

*Gessy Alvarez earned her MFA from Columbia University and is the recipient of scholarships from Columbia University, the Fine Arts Work Center, and the Aspen Writers' Foundation, as well as, artist residencies at the Kimmel Harding Nelson Center for the Arts and the Millay Colony for the Arts, where she was a Mid Atlantic Arts Foundation Creative Fellow. She is an alum of the Voices at VONA Workshop and the Bread Loaf Writers' Conference. She interviews writers and poets at her blog, *Digging Through the Fat*, and is at work on a collection of short prose.

Morgan Baker teaches at Emerson College, where she received the Stanzler Award for Excellence in Teaching. Her work has appeared in *Talking Writing, Brain, Child Magazine, The Boston Globe, The New York Times Magazine, The Martha's Vineyard Times* and elsewhere. She is the mother of two grown daughters and lives with her husband and two Portuguese Water Dogs near Boston.

Jason Lee Brown is the author of the novel, *Prowler: The Mad Gasser of Mattoon*, and the poetry chapbook, *Blue Collar Fathers*. He is the Series Editor of *New Stories from The Midwest* and a contributing editor of *River Styx*. His writing has appeared in numerous literary journals, most recently the *Kenyon Review, Literary Review, North American Review, The Journal, Southern Humanities Review, Ecotone,* and *Crab Orchard Review*. He earned a Master of Fine Arts in Creative Writing from Southern Illinois University Carbondale.

Sarah Cooper hails from Clemson, South Carolina where she teaches literature at Clemson University. She has recent publications in *Shot Glass Journal, Sling Magazine* and *Wild Age Press*. Her passion is self-improvement and when she's not writing she's working out her body as an owner and operator of a local CrossFit box.

*Amber Dermont received her MFA in fiction from the University of Iowa Writers' Workshop. Her short stories have appeared in numerous literary magazines and anthologies, including Dave Eggers's *Best American Nonrequired Reading 2005*, Francis Ford Coppola's *Zoetrope: All-Story*, and Jane Smiley's *Best New American Voices 2006*. A graduate of Vassar College, she received her Ph.D. in creative writing and literature from the University of Houston. She currently serves as an associate professor of English and creative writing at Rice University in Houston, TX and is the author of the story collection *Damage Control* and the novel *The Starboard Sea*.

Litsa Dremousis is the author of *Altitude Sickness* (Future Tense Books). Seattle Metropolitan Magazine named *Altitude Sickness* one of the all-time "20 Books Every Seattleite Must Read". Her essay "After the Fire" was selected as one of the "Most Notable Essays of 2011" by Best American Essays 2012, she's a Contributing Editor at *The Weeklings*, and *The Seattle Weekly* named her one of "50 Women Who Rock Seattle". Her work appears in *The Believer, BlackBook, Esquire, Jezebel, McSweeney's, Men's Health, Monkeybicycle, MSN, New York Magazine, Nerve, Nylon, The Onion's A.V. Club, Paste, Poets & Writers, Salon, Slate, The Weeklings*, on NPR, KUOW, and additional venues. She has interviewed Sherman Alexie, The Black Keys, Betty Davis (the legendary, reclusive soul singer), Death Cab for Cutie, Estelle, Ron Jeremy, Janelle Monae, Alanis Morissette, Kelly Rowland, Wanda Sykes, Rufus Wainwright, Ann Wilson and several dozen others. @LitsaDremousis, litsadremousis.com.

*Max Garland, Poet Laureate of Wisconsin 2013-2014, is a former rural letter carrier and author of *The Postal Confessions*, winner of the Juniper Prize, and *Hunger Wide as Heaven*, which won the Cleveland State Poetry Center Open Competition, as well as a chapbook *Apparition*. His work has appeared in *Poetry*, *New England Review*, *Gettysburg Review*, *Best American Short Stories*, and other journals and anthologies. He has received a NEA Fellowship for Poetry, Michener Fiction Fellowship, a Bush Literary Fellowship, the Tara Short Fiction Prize, and fellowships from the Wisconsin Arts Board in both poetry and fiction. He lives and teaches in Eau Claire, WI.

Jen Gaskell is a wife, mom, business professional, writer, singer, runner, and yogi. She lives in a small town in Wisconsin on beautiful Lake Michigan with her husband and two young daughters. Jen is a co-producer/co-director of *Listen To Your Mother Show Milwaukee*. Jen's writing is a regular contributor to *Postpartum Progress*, and her writing can also be found on her blog *Tranquila Mama*.

Amy Hassinger is the author of three novels: *Nina: Adolescence* (Putnam 2003), *The Priest's Madonna* (Putnam 2006), and the forthcoming *After the Dam* (Red Hen Press 2016). Her writing has been translated into Dutch, Spanish, Portuguese, Russian, and Indonesian and has won awards from *Creative Nonfiction*, *Publisher's Weekly*, and the Illinois Arts Council. Her work has appeared in *Creative Nonfiction*, *The Writers' Chronicle*, *The Los Angeles Review of Books* and other publications. She earned her M.F.A. from the Iowa Writers' Workshop and serves as a Faculty Mentor in the University of Nebraska's low-residency MFA in Writing Program. She teaches regularly at the Osher Lifelong Learning Institute at the University of Illinois and has been leading writing workshops in the Champaign-Urbana area since 2013.

*****Carolyn Healy** is a therapist-turned-writer who has invested hundreds of hours listening to people as they rewrite their life stories. While her interests include serious things like grief, resilience and transformative change, her vantage point allows her to address them with insight and a certain dark humor. A lifelong Chicagoan, she grew up the only child of a single mom, which fueled her curiosity about how other people live, and strengthened her backbone. She has been a columnist for her local newspaper and is writing a book on finding the hidden gifts in grieving. She has also written three guided journals and a guide to writing a legacy letter/ethical will. Carolyn blogs at www.chicagonow.com/mscrankypants and her website on grieving is www.wavesofgrief.com.

Jody Hobbs Hesler lives and writes in the foothills of the Blue Ridge Mountains. Her fiction, feature articles, essays, and book reviews appear or are forthcoming in *Gargoyle, The Georgia Review, Sequestrum, [PANK], Steel Toe Review, Valparaiso Fiction Review, Prime Number, Pearl, A Short Ride: Remembering Barry Hannah* (VOX Press), *Charlottesville Family Magazine,* and several regional prize anthologies and other publications. One of her stories has received a nomination for a Pushcart Prize. She has been a fellow at Virginia Center for the Creative Arts, and, currently, she is an MFA candidate at Lesley University. You can find out more about her writing at jodyhobbshesler.com.

Jennifer Highland's poetry has appeared in *Heron Tree, Festival of Language, Josephine Quarterly, Quiddity,* and elsewhere. She practices osteopathy in New Hampshire's first solar-powered medical office.

Liam Hogan was abandoned in a library at the tender age of 3, only to emerge blinking into the sunlight many years later, with a head full of words and an aversion to loud noises. His work has been performed at Liars' League, and you can find it in print in #Alice150 anthology 'Beware the Little White Rabbit' (Leap Books) and in Sci-Phi Journal. Or http:// happyendingnotguaranteed.blogspot.co.uk/ if you like that sort of thing. He dreams in Dewey Decimals.

Kathy Lanzarotti lives in Delafield, WI with her husband and four daughters. She won the Wisconsin Writers Association's Jade Ring contest for short fiction with her story, "Have You Seen Me?", which appears in this anthology. She is currently enrolled in the MA in writing program at Mt. Mary University.

Katie Manning is the author of three poetry chapbooks, including *The Gospel of the Bleeding Woman*. She has received *The Nassau Review* Author Award for Poetry, and she is the founding Editor-in-Chief of *Whale Road Review*. She is an assistant professor of writing at Point Loma Nazarene University in San Diego, where she collects books, tea, board games, and sea shells. Find her online at www.katiemanningpoet.com.

Mel Miskimen is a regular contributor for *More* magazine and *The Huffington Post*. Her memoir *Sit. Stay. Heal.* is a heartwarming, inspiring story of grappling with loss, finding hope, and healing with the help of a badly behaved Labrador retriever. "It's sort of a *Tuesdays With Morrie* meets *Marley and Me*." It will be published in 2016 by Sourcebooks. Her essays have been published in *Wisconsin Trails*, *Fetch*, and *Rosebud Literary Magazine*. She's a past winner of the Wisconsin Regional Writer's Jade Ring and Florence Lindemann awards and a frequent essayist for Milwaukee Public Radio and a storyteller for The Moth. She is represented by the Kathy Green Literary Agency.

Pam Parker's short fiction, poetry and essays have appeared in numerous print and electronic journals, including *Potomac Review, Grey Sparrow Press, The MacGuffin* and more. She is a regular contributor to "Lake Effect" on Milwaukee Public Radio. Her work has earned accolades from the Wisconsin Broadcaster's Association, Wisconsin Writers Association and the Wisconsin Academy of Sciences, Arts and Letters. She makes her home in Wauwatosa, WI with her husband, though her heart is often in western Massachusetts or Glasgow, Scotland. To read some of her work, find links at pamwrites.net.

*Tony Press lives near San Francisco and sometimes pays attention. His fiction, non-fiction and poetry have appeared in *BorderSenses*; *Boston Literary*; *5×5*; *Doorknobs & BodyPaint*; *Foundling Review*; *Grey Sparrow Journal*; *Halfway Down the Stairs*; *JMWW*; *Literary Orphans*; *MacGuffin*; *Menda City Review*; Naugatuck River Review; *Rio Grande Review*; *Riverbabble*; *SFWP Journal*; *Switchback*; *Toasted Cheese*; Turning Wheel; and others.

Diana Raab, Ph.D., is a memoirist, poet, blogger and transpersonal psychologist. Her educational background includes health administration, nursing, creative writing and psychology. She's an award-winning author of eight books, over 500 articles and poems, and editor of two anthologies, *Writers on the Edge: 22 Writers Speak About Addiction and Dependency*, and *Writers and Their Notebooks*. Raab's two memoirs are *Regina's Closet: Finding My Grandmother's Secret Journal* and *Healing With Words: A Writer's Cancer Journey*. She has 4 poetry collections, the latest is called, *Lust*. She is a regular blogger for *Psychology Today, Huffington Post (Huff50), BrainSpeak, and PsychAlive.*

Alexandra Rosas is a contributing author to the HerStories Project as well as other anthologies. Voted a Babble Top 100 Mom and a BlogHer Voice of The Year pick four years running, her writing has appeared at *The Huffington Post*, Queen Latifah's website and BlogHer. Alexandra proudly presents with the

TheMoth's National Live StoryTeller's Tour and is co-producer of the Listen To Your Mother Show Milwaukee. She lives with her husband and three children in Wisconsin. She is a regular columnist with *Purple Clover* and writes on her personal blog Good Day Regular People. Find her on twitter as @gdrpempress.

Mike Smith has published three collections of poetry, including *Multiverse,* a collection of two anagrammatic cycles. His essay, "Shadow Texts," is part of a book-length manuscript which documents the strange set of coincidences surrounding the death of his first wife, Emily, five months after the birth of their second child, and the similar diagnosis of his stepdaughter, also named Emily, three years later. Recent poems and essays have appeared in or are forthcoming in December: *The Edgar Allan Poe Review, The Greensboro Review, Image: Journal of Art and Faith, Notre Dame Magazine, The Sun,* and *Witness.* In addition, his translation of the first part of Goethe's *Faust* was published by Shearsman Books in 2012. Read more about him at https://mikesmithmultiverse.wordpress.com

Carol Wobig spent a few years in a convent and many more years working in a pizza factory before she retired and started writing. She won the Florence Lindemann Humor Contest, and Honorable Mentions in the *Lorian Hemingway Short Story Contest,* and in two *Writer's Digest* competitions. Her monologues were performed in community theater, and her stories have been published in the following journals: *Grey Sparrow, Clapboard House, Persimmon Tree* and *Rosebud.* She is the author of *Poached Is Not an Option.*

Dallas Woodburn is a Steinbeck Fellow in Creative Writing at San Jose State University. A three-time Pushcart Prize nominee, she won second place in the American Fiction Prize and her work is forthcoming in *American Fiction Volume 13: The Best Unpublished Short Stories by American Writers* (New

Rivers Press). Her short story collection was a finalist for the 2012 Flannery O'Connor Award for Short Fiction; individual pieces have appeared in *The Nashville Review, Superstition Review, Louisiana Literature, Monkeybicycle,* and *Ayris,* among others. Her nonfiction has been published in *The Los Angeles Times, Family Circle, Prime Number,* and *Passages North.* She has been honored with the international Glass Woman Prize, the Brian Mexicott Playwriting Award, and a merit scholarship to attend the Key West Literary Seminar. A former fiction editor of *Sycamore Review,* she also served as editor of the anthology *Dancing With The Pen: a collection of today's best youth writing.*

*Member of editorial review board

Beyond the Book - Resources

Know someone struggling with the darkness of depression? Has a story, essay or poem in *Done Darkness* caused you to think more about your struggles or someone else's? We've compiled a brief list of resources for our readers in the United States and encourage you to reach out if you need help. These resources are accurate at the time we are going to press. Please check your local area too.

SUICIDE PREVENTION
National Suicide Prevention Lifeline   1-800-273-TALK (8255)
American Foundation for Suicide Prevention (links to local resources): https://www.afsp.org
Suicide Awareness Voices of Education http://www.save.org

DEPRESSION
NAMI: National Alliance on Mental Illness Helpline
1-800-950-6264

https://www.nami.org/#

NIMH: National Institute of Mental Health
https://www.nimh.nih.gov/index.shtml
(Note: The NIMH offers numerous online fact sheets about depression, postpartum depression, bipolar disorder, seasonal affective disorder and more.)

Acknowledgments

This book has been a labor of love and we owe thanks to so, so many. Special love goes out first of all to our beloved Red Oak Writing in Milwaukee, WI which has helped both of us on our writing journeys. Red Oak is directed by the talented and generous Kim Suhr. Kim, Kathy and Pam all met in a *Shut up! & Write* class, offered by Milwaukee's writing guru, Judy Bridges, the founder of Red Bird Studios. To say we are grateful to both Judy and Kim doesn't feel like quite enough. We count ourselves blessed to call both of them mentors and friends.

We are grateful to our brave authors, those in the book and those whose work did not make the cut. We had to make difficult choices and many worthy pieces could not be included. Helping us with those choices were the gracious members of our editorial board, amazing authors and poets all, Gessy Alvarez, Amber Dermont, Max Garland, Carolyn Healy, Tony Press and Carol Wobig. So many thanks to each of them! For helpful conversations and advice, we are grateful to Amy Lou Jenkins and Ann Angel, both fabulous Milwaukee area authors.

We owe a huge debt of gratitude to Shannon Ishizaki and our team at Orange Hat Publishing, especially Christina Schuler.

To our families, near, far and gone on, we are thankful for support, encouragement and love. And to our readers, thank you for encouraging an open conversation about depression and breaking through the silent barriers and stigma about mental imbalances.